11–17

Death of an Englishman

ALSO BY MAGDALEN NABB

Death of a Dutchman
Death in Springtime
Death in Autumn
The Marshal and the Murderer
The Marshal and the Madwoman
The Marshal's Own Case
The Marshal Makes His Report
The Marshal at the Villa Torrini
Property of Blood
Some Bitter Taste
The Innocent
Vita Nuova
The Monster of Florence

WITH PAOLO VAGHEGGI

The Prosecutor

DEATH OF AN ENGLISHMAN

MAGDALEN NABB

SOHO
CRIME

Although set very specifically in Florence,
which it lovingly portrays, all the characters and events in
this story are entirely fictitious and no resemblance is
intended to any real person, either living or dead.

✛

First published in Great Britain in 1981
Copyright © 1981 by Magdalen Nabb and © 1999
by Diogenes Verlag AG Zurich

Published in the United States in 2001 by
Soho Press, Inc.
853 Broadway
New York, NY 10003

Library of Congress Cataloging-in-Publication Data
Nabb, Magdalen, 1947–2007
Death of an Englishman / Magdalen Nabb.

p. cm.
ISBN 978-1-61695-299-0
eISBN 978-1-56947-820-2
1. Guarnaccia, Marshal (Fictitious character)—Fiction.
2. Police—Italy—Florence—Fiction. 3. Florence (Italy)—Fiction.
I. Title.
PR6064.A18 D4 2001
823'.914—dc21   2001020654

Printed in the United States of America
10 9 8 7 6 5 4 3 2 1

Part One

CHAPTER 1

THE SMALL OFFICE WAS in darkness, except where the red night lamp stood by the telephone on the desk, and the white kid gloves lying on top of a sheaf of papers within the patch of light were flushed pink. A black uniform jacket was hung over the back of a swivel chair and a matching military great-coat, lined with red, was buttoned neatly on to a hanger behind the door, alongside a well-brushed hat. There was just room in the office for a camp bed along one white-painted wall, and on the camp bed, his legs carefully placed so as not to crease the red stripe down his trousers, lay Carabiniere Bacci. He was doing night duty. The features of his Florentine face were serene. He was asleep.

He was very young and he slept deeply, with a copy of the *Codice di Procedura Penale* open on his chest and a handbook of military tactics on the floor beside him. His idea had been to stay awake all night and study, but the closeness of the little office, the softness of the red light, and the silence had combined to close his brown eyes, though he thought in his dream that he was still reading.

The telephone shrilled loudly and insistently in its pool of light. Carabiniere Bacci had leapt to his feet before he was awake and saluted before he was on his feet. When he realized what the noise was, he grabbed the receiver quickly before it could wake the Marshal. A small, distressed voice said:

'Marshal Guarnaccia, Marshal . . . you'd better come round here right away, it's the Englishman, he—'

'Just a moment.' Carabiniere Bacci felt about for the main light switch and picked up a pencil.

'Marshal?'

'This is not Marshal Guarnaccia, this is Carabiniere Bacci speaking, who's that?'

There was a pause, then the voice continued obediently, 'Cipolla, Gianpaolo Maria.'

'And the address?'

'My address?' The voice was so weak that Carabiniere Bacci wondered if he were speaking to a man or a boy.

'Your address and the address you're speaking from if they're different.'

'Via Romana eighty-three red, that's my address.'

'And you're speaking from?'

'Via Maggio fifty-eight.'

'And there's been a crime committed there?'

'Yes, it's the Englishman . . . Is the Marshal not there? My sister lives next door to the Marshal, with her husband being a gardener in the Boboli, so I know him—and the Marshal . . .'

'Might I ask you,' said Carabiniere Bacci with all the cold dignity of his two months' practical experience, 'just what you're doing in Via Maggio in the middle of the night if you live down Via Romana?'

Another pause. Then the small voice said, 'But . . . it's morning . . . I work here.'

'I see. Well. Stay where you are and I'll be over there in five minutes.' Carabiniere Bacci pulled on his jacket and greatcoat and adjusted his hat and kid gloves carefully. It distressed him not to wash and shave but the matter might be urgent . . . he hesitated, looking toward the door that led to the Marshal's living quarters and then back at the door where his coat had hung and where a Beretta nine was now visible, hung up with its white leather holster and webbing.

The Marshal was sweating in bed with the onset of flu, which was why Carabiniere Bacci had insisted on sleeping in the office instead of going upstairs to bed—quite unnecessarily, in the Marshal's opinion—but Carabiniere Bacci was known as the 'perfect student.' Quietly he took down the gun, checked it and strapped it on with an eye on the inner door. He ought to wake the Marshal, perhaps, or phone through to Borgo Ognissanti in case he needed help . . . but if he phoned Headquarters they would surely tell him to stay where he was and they'd send an Officer . . . Carabiniere Bacci had never in his life been near the scene of a crime . . . still . . . he was drumming softly with his gloved fingers on the desk. The Marshal had said that if anything important came up—it might not be anything at all, of course—nothing ever did happen at Stazione Pitti . . .

Carabiniere Bacci did not like the Marshal. In the first place because he was Sicilian and he suspected him of being, if not actually Mafia, at least *mafioso*, and he knew that the Marshal knew of his suspicion and even encouraged it. He seemed to think it was funny. He disliked the Marshal in the second place because he was too large and fat and had an embarrassing eye complaint—embarrassing to Carabiniere Bacci—that caused him to weep copiously during the hours of sunlight. And since he continually mourned the absence of his wife and children who were at home in Syracuse, his rolling tears often seemed distressingly real—distressing to Carabiniere Bacci. The Marshal himself would fish unperturbedly for the dark glasses that were always in one of his voluminous pockets and explain to anyone and everyone, 'It's all right, just a complaint I have. It's the sunshine starts it off.'

He thought he wouldn't wake the Marshal. Via Maggio was only two steps away. He could be there and back in ten minutes and then wake him if it seemed necessary. He stepped outside and locked the office door.

The caller had been right—it was morning, just about. A sluggish, damp December dawn. Thick yellow fog rose off the river and seeped along the narrow streets to deaden Carabiniere Bacci's footsteps as he came out under the dark, stone archway and crossed the sloping forecourt of the Pitti palace. The few ghostly cars that had been left there all night were misted with fine droplets of moisture. He crossed the silent piazza and cut through an alley that slit the high buildings dividing Piazza Pitti from Via Maggio. He was shivering inside his heavy greatcoat, aware of the whole city sleeping behind closed shutters. The streetlights were still on, but since the narrow passage had only one iron lamp at each end, Carabiniere Bacci had to tread carefully, squeezing past the inevitable line of illegally parked mopeds, his nose discreetly lifted against the stench of drains that hung in the dawn fog and that would not be dispersed until the rush-hour traffic drove it off and replaced it with exhaust fumes. Halfway along the alley, at its gloomiest point, he stumbled on to a Coca-Cola can that rolled away along the uneven flags, rattling his nerves. When he came out in Via Maggio he stopped, wondering which way to go. To his right, the street of tall Renaissance palaces went along to the river and the Santa Trinita bridge, invisible now in the fog; to his left, a shorter stretch of the street led to a tiny triangular piazza where it met the road coming from the Pitti. Consulting both the red and black numbering systems carefully, Carabiniere Bacci turned left toward the little piazza and crossed over . . . 52 . . . 106 red . . . 108 red . . . the faint old red numbers were barely visible in the gray half-light but the large black ones stood out clearly on their white plates and it was a black one he was looking for . . . 54 . . . 110 red . . . 56 . . . 58. There was an indecipherable coat of arms carved in stone at first-floor level. The gigantic, iron-studded doors reached up to the coat of arms, and the shutters on all three upper floors were closed. No thread of light was showing to indicate which floor the call had come from and Carabiniere Bacci realized now that he had forgotten to ask what name to look for. There was a bank housed in the ground floor of the building and a shop with its metal shutter down. The shop marked the end of Via Maggio and faced the little piazza. It was the shop which eventually reminded him—an Englishman—he'd read it somewhere . . . 'A nation of shopkeepers' . . . he ran a white-gloved finger delicately down the polished brass bellplate, peering closely at the list of names . . . Frediani . . . Cipriani . . . Cesarini . . . no . . . A. Langley-Smythe, that would be it on the ground-floor right—but surely not the ground floor? The nameplate on the bell opposite was blank, must be a porter's lodge. Up on the top floor left was another English name: 'Miss E. White,' with, in brackets, 'Landor.' But the caller had certainly said a man. He rang the ground-floor bell. No answer. He rang again, bending to put his ear to the speaker. Nothing. It could be a hoax . . . or even a trap of some sort, it often happened . . . he'd heard stories . . . he was getting a little nervous. It could be some Sicilian who had it in for the Marshal . . . *or terrorists!* 'Nothing ever happens at Stazione Pitti,' he repeated to himself quietly, and then he heard footsteps. They seemed near but they couldn't be coming from inside the building, nothing could be heard beyond those doors. The footsteps were coming round the corner beyond the shop, slow, heavy steps. A dark figure emerged from the fog; it was the private night guard on his round.

'Open up for me,' demanded Carabiniere Bacci when the guard reached him. 'There's something wrong in here.'

'Nothing wrong when I last passed,' said the guard

phlegmatically, pushing back his cap. He selected a key from the rattling bunch in his hand, unlocked one of the great doors and leaned on it with his shoulder enough to open it a couple of feet. He tossed in the white ticket that proved to the residents that he had done his round, then stood back. His radio coughed suddenly into life and just as suddenly silenced itself with a whistle.

'And is that all you did on your last round?' asked Carabiniere Bacci severely.

'No. I went up in the lift and checked every door. You'll find a ticket in every one if you're going in there. But since you're here I'll leave you to it this time.'

'You could come in on your next round . . . I might want you to take a message . . .' Carabiniere Bacci wished again that he'd had time to shave. He felt less confident than when he'd first stepped out of the office.

'I'm off home,' said the guard. 'My last round. Bank guard should be here at eight.' He walked on with deliberate steps, selected another key and vanished into the next big door-way. Well, the bank guard, when he came, was sure to be an ex-carabiniere and more helpful. Carabiniere Bacci pushed at the studded oak with his shoulder until the door opened enough to admit him.

A wide, stone-flagged passage, ill-lit by a tiny night-light, led to a pair of high, wooden carriage gates which would presumably open on to the central courtyard of the building. Carabiniere Bacci felt for a switch and turned on a marginally stronger bulb hanging in a spiked iron lantern before the gates. To his right was the staff entrance to the bank, to his left a disused porter's lodge with the inquiry window boarded up. Walking slowly and loudly on the flagged floor, he reached the locked gates and followed a smaller passage round to the left where a wide stone staircase led to the upper floors. At the bottom of the staircase, on the left, were the tenants' letter-boxes, on the right, a lift and a door which looked as if it might lead to a storeroom. A crack of yellow light was showing round this door. The name on the bell was A. Langley-Smythe. Carabiniere Bacci's loud footfall stopped. With one gloved finger he pushed gently on the door until it swung open. A parchment lamp was lit on a dusty, littered desk. Beyond it the room was gloomy and he didn't see A. Langley-Smythe at first. He did see, sitting by the lamp in an upright chair as if he were on guard, a tiny, ashen-faced man with a brush of spiky hair and a black cotton overall.

'So why the devil didn't you wake me up? Oh, did you? Well, you thought wrong—you took what? Carabiniere Bacci, I will personally . . . Have you touched anything? For God's sake, don't touch anything!—Who? what's he doing there . . . Just a minute, I've got to get a . . . atchoo! He doesn't just look in a state of shock, he *is* in a state of shock. His wife's on her deathbed, may even have died last night; his sister's down at Via Romana so what's he doing—Look, just keep him there till I arrive, I'll have to phone through to Borgo Ognissanti first—and *don't touch anything* . . . Oh Lord . . .' He rang Headquarters.

Marshal Guarnaccia struggled slowly into his uniform, sneezing almost continuously. He felt sick and dizzy and his whole body burned and ached. He found some aspirin in the bathroom and took half a dozen of them with four tumblers of mineral water that left his throat as hot and dry as when he started. Tomorrow he should be going home for Christmas; he couldn't be ill, he couldn't spend Christmas alone and sick in his quarters in Florence, when every other Sicilian in the city was elbowing his way on to one of the overflowing southbound trains, laden with lumpy parcels and suitcases tied up with string. He sneezed again loudly and stepped out under the archway, feeling light-headed as the cold damp-ness enveloped his feverish face. A watery sun was just breaking through the morning fog and Marshal Guarnaccia began to weep. Sighing, he delved into his coat pocket and put on a pair of dark glasses.

The Englishman's flat, when the Marshal reached it, was as busy as a railway station. There were more than a dozen people inside and two porters from the Medico-Legal Institute were leaning in the doorway arguing heatedly with the Brigadier on guard.

'I can't digest it and that's that . . .'

'It's the temperature of the oil that counts, if you tried it the way my mother makes it . . .'

'As far as I'm concerned a good beefsteak . . .'

The Marshal pushed past them with a nod. 'Jesus, Mary and Joseph,' he said softly, once inside. He wasn't looking at the body of A. Langley-Smythe which, anyway, was hidden from his view by two photographers, the Substitute Prosecutor and Professor Forli from the Medico-Legal Institute, he was looking out into the courtyard at the pathetic figure of the little cleaner in his skimpy black overall. A french window had, in some recent decade, been let into the thick stone wall, and the cleaner was out there picking up bits of rubbish from the mossy flags around big terra-cotta plantpots and putting them in a polythene bag. His face had a greenish pallor.

'He looked as though he might faint if he waited in here any longer,' explained Carabiniere Bacci, who had not been far from fainting himself during the time he had been alone with the body. 'Apparently, he cleans the courtyard once a month as well as the stairs and entrance which he does every week. I thought it might take his mind off things since he had to wait . . . and as you said his wife was ill . . .'

'She's dead,' murmured the Marshal, his great eyes fixed on the stooping figure outside. He had taken the time to call next door on his way out and the gardener had opened up, his eyes red, his face dark with beard. He had been preparing breakfast for the children, as his wife was still down at Via Romana.

The group round the body was breaking up. The Captain from Headquarters who was in charge of the case came out of the bedroom, where his technicians were working, and regarded the Substitute Prosecutor with a raised eyebrow. The other turned his own eyes heavenward. There was no need to say it. That this had to happen so near the holidays . . .

'And no chance of its being a suicide,' sighed the S.P.

'Hardly. Shot in the back and no weapon found.'

'Well, do what you can . . .'

Do what you can to clear it up by Christmas. The S.P. shook hands with the Captain and with Professor Forli who was also ready to leave and was closing his bag. The Marshal turned and looked at him hopefully:

'D'you think you could—'

'Nothing,' said the Professor automatically. 'Not until after the autopsy—other than what you can see for yourself. And then a lot will depend on our knowing what time he last ate . . . Let's hope he eats in a restaurant—it seems likely, he was obviously a bachelor.' The Professor, an elegant, gray-haired man, glanced at the prevailing squalor around him with evident distaste.

'Actually,' said the Marshal humbly, 'that's all a bit beyond my scope,' and he sat down heavily on a dusty antique chair and mopped his brow. 'I was going to ask you if you could give me anything for this fever.'

'Flu?'

'I suppose so.'

'What have you been taking?'

'Just aspirin.'

The Professor felt his pulse. 'You ought to be in bed.'

'I know.' The Marshal's glance went involuntarily to Carabiniere Bacci, rising and falling gently on his well-polished heels by the french windows and slapping himself nervously with his kid gloves.

'I see.' The Professor had followed his glance.

'And I've a Brigadier off sick and my only other boy's already on his way home.' It was the same everywhere at holiday times, the inexorable trickle southwards, as steady and as inevitable as sand running through an egg-timer, leaving museums, hospitals, banks and police stations severely understaffed.

'We're in the same boat,' sympathized the Professor. 'I'll prescribe an antibiotic—but I warn you, you'd better take it easy. Let the lad do your running about and leave this business to the Captain.'

'You needn't worry about that. Stolen handbags are about our limit at Pitti; he won't want me. I'm just keeping an eye on this boy. The sooner he's safely back in Officer School the better. They seem to come younger every year. I must be getting old.'

'Well, try and get some rest, anyway, and drink plenty of fluids.' Both of them noticed at the same time the almost empty whiskey bottle standing by the parchment lamp. 'Not that stuff.'

'I've never tasted it.' The Marshal drank half a litre of red every day with his evening meal, never more nor less, and a drop of *vinsanto* on Sundays.

'And no wine, either, while you're on this.' The Professor was reading the Marshal's mind as he wrote. He passed him the prescription and gave a pat to the enormous shoulder. 'Bear up.'

'Captain . . . ?' One of the technicians was crouching in a corner of the room, examining some object there. The Captain went over to look. A blue and white majolica bust, the head of an angel. The technician was gently brushing away some dust to reveal a piece of string encircling the neck.

'Oh no . . .' said the Captain softly. He didn't relish the complications this was going to cause.

''Fraid so, sir . . .' He pulled on the string and brought its lead seal into view.

The Captain stood up. 'Get someone over from Pitti, will you? Try Doctor Biondini, the director of the Palatine gallery, he should be there at this time. He'll probably be able to tell you something immediately, but if not, ring me at my office as soon as you hear . . .'

When the Captain had gone back to the bedroom, Carabiniere Bacci went over to the crouching figure and asked timidly: 'What's happened?' He looked at the small lead seal. 'What does it mean?'

'Trouble,' said the technician. 'Rome . . .' As if the two were synonymous. '*Can I have the lights over here?* Try and keep out of the way, lad, will you . . .'

'CAN WE shift him yet?' The porters had been hanging about for over an hour and a half. The floor outside the flat was littered with cigarette ends and their conversation was becoming desultory.

'With the fillet on it, mind you, and rare. Nothing with it except maybe a dish of shallots done in plenty of butter, sweet and sour.'

'Onions make me ill, I never touch them.'

'You can take him,' said the Professor, hurrying out to

catch up with the Substitute Prosecutor and invite him to
breakfast in a bar.

The porters began to manoeuvre the considerable bulk of
A. Langley-Smythe on to their stretcher, and the Marshal
noticed that he was wearing trousers under his dressing-gown
and that there was not a lot of blood, although a small patch
of it had trickled on to the corner of a Persian carpet that lay
before the fireplace. The porters left with their burden, their
loud voices echoing in the stone passageway. The Captain
and his men were closeted in the bedroom again, where they
seemed to have found something of interest. The Marshal
and Carabiniere Bacci were left alone in the living-room.

'Carabiniere Bacci.'

'Yes, sir?'

The Marshal's eyes were closed, his large, damp hands
placed squarely on his knees as if to keep himself steady. 'I
want you to do one thing immediately. Do it properly and do
it quickly.'

'Yes sir.' Carabiniere Bacci clicked to attention on the
stone floor. Flinching slightly, the Marshal handed him the
prescription and said: 'Go out into the piazza, to the chemist
next to the stationer's, and get this filled.'

'Yes, sir.' Carabiniere Bacci drew on his gloves, took the
prescription delicately between two fingers and strode elegantly toward the door.

'And be quick about it!'

'Yessir!'

The Marshal sat where he was, his large watery eyes open
now but expressionless, taking in everything around him.
The room was overfurnished, in a strangely haphazard fashion, and dusty rather than dirty, the sort of claustrophobic
dustiness of attics and junkrooms. The furniture was a mot-
ley collection of styles and periods, all of it very antique and

much of it too large even in such a high, spacious room as this one. There were some oil paintings that hadn't been hung, just propped against the walls on top of the furniture. The only pieces that looked settled there were the desk and the worn leather chairs before and behind it, on one of which the Marshal was now sitting, and an enormous old armchair, upholstered in faded red velvet. The velvet cushions were squashed into somebody's habitual sitting position and an English newspaper was half pushed down the side of the seat. The chair was by the stone fireplace where the remains of a wood fire lay cold in the grate. The hearth was littered with cigarette ends. The Marshal was tempted to sink his aching limbs into the velvet cushions but the imprint of the Englishman's body was too evident. He sighed and went on looking around him. 'Very nice,' he said softly, regarding the marble statuary on either side of the fireplace. The two figures, their deep folds heavily accented by dust, looked Roman but they might have been Florentine copies. Very nice, even so. A rich man, then, but living on the ground floor . . . he stared out again at the empty courtyard, his great bulk as still and his great eyes as sightless as those of the marble figures.

'Boh!' He thumped the padded arm of his chair, raising a little cloud of dust, and heaved himself up to take a look in the bathroom. The place hadn't been cleaned for some time. Dirty underwear was lying in the bidet and on the floor. There were lumps of toothpaste and grayish patches of shaving lather around the sink and a rusty streak down the bath where the tap was dripping steadily. Automatically, the Marshal tried to turn it off but without success.

'Marshal?'

'In here.' There was a faint but unmistakable smell of vomit.

Carabiniere Bacci stood in the doorway holding a white package. His bright brown eyes took in the state of the bathroom, but he said nothing except: 'Shall I keep the keys?'

'No—yes, the Captain will want them, I suppose.'

While waiting for the Captain they glanced into the kitchen. There were used coffee cups in the sink, a small coffee-maker on the spattered stove. A fridge contained a small box of milk and half a packet of slightly rancid butter. In a metal cupboard they found a jar of freshly ground coffee, English jam, expensive plain biscuits.

'Old England Stores,' said Carabiniere Bacci, 'In Via Vecchietti.'

The Marshal looked at him.

'That's where he would buy these things.' He blushed. 'My mother sometimes buys tea there.'

'Tea?'

'Yes.'

'*Tea?*'

'They have their own blend.' Carabiniere Bacci's face was scarlet but he had no intention of trying to explain the historical Florentine predilection for all things English. He reached down a cannister from the corner of the cupboard. 'Old England Breakfast Tea.'

'Hmph,' said the Marshal.

'Shall we go?' suggested the Captain from the doorway. It was only after he had given the keys to the guard on the door and instructed him to lock up after the technicians that anyone noticed the small figure waiting patiently in the shadows, along the flagged passageway.

'Cipolla,' murmured the Marshal in the Captain's ear. 'The cleaner who found him. His wife died last night so if you could—'

'I see. Come along to Pitti with us, will you? The Marshal will take a statement from you—come on, come on! Put down that bag of rubbish and let's go.'

'It's not rubbish, Marshal.' The little man was afraid to address the Captain personally. 'It's the stuff from the court-yard, things that people drop from their windows and terraces . . . clothes-pegs mostly and children's toys, and bits of washing sometimes . . .'

'Put it down,' said the Marshal gently, 'wherever you usually put it, and come along with us. We'll get you a coffee and grappa on the way, you look as though you need it.'

The little man hung his polythene bag on a hook by the lift door where the tenants would collect their belongings, and followed them out, blinking, into the damp, noisy morning. The Marshal put on his dark glasses. The bar on the corner of the little triangular piazza was still busy, its glass counter piled high with breakfast sandwiches and brioches, the coffee-machine steaming non-stop.

'What can I give you, Marshal? Three coffees, is it?'

'Four.' The little cleaner refused to eat anything; the others bought brioches but the Marshal couldn't swallow his. He was too hot and feeling worse by the minute. They stood at the counter near the steamy warmth, gazing out of the open door at a long white coach from Germany that was carrying Christmas shoppers and had got itself wedged across the triangle, unable to negotiate the scattering of illegally parked cars in the center of it. The driver must have come along by the Pitti and then tried to make the sharp turn back into Via Maggio to make for the river. The cars he was holding up, some of them far out of sight, were blasting their horns in fury while a patiently despairing *vigile* in a tall white helmet tried to help him back up without breaking a shop window, and to persuade the owners of the parked vehicles to come out of the bar and move them.

'Can't even have breakfast in peace in this city,' remarked one of the latter loudly, dabbing delicately at his mouth with a paper napkin and ostentatiously taking his time.

'Have a bit of patience, can't you?' pleaded the young *vigile*, looking in from the doorway.

Those shopkeepers who had no customers, and some who had, came out to watch the familiar spectacle. The dignified, gray-haired stationer stood with his hands behind his back, shaking his head slowly at the disorder. The Neapolitan meat-roaster, to whom the stationer did not speak, mopped his brow on a stained white apron and grinned gold-toothily, the flames of his wood fire flickering diabolically behind him. The jeweller watched beside his Alsatian dog. Normally, the Marshal would have been in the best of spirits, murder or no murder, at being out in the piazza enjoying the mingled smells of woodsmoke and roasting beef, coffee and toast, instead of being shut in his office at Pitti. But today the noise and confusion made his head spin and he was relieved when they paid for their coffee and left. The Captain's car was on the sloping forecourt.

'Wait for me here,' he told the driver, 'I shall want to go back to Headquarters in about fifteen minutes.' As they walked on he told the Marshal, 'You'll need to inform the British Consulate, they'll get in touch with his next of kin, if he has any—and you might send your Carabiniere to the English church and library for me—somebody should know something about him . . .'

The main doors of the Pitti were open now and a few winter tourists and school parties were going through the central courtyard to the galleries and the Boboli Gardens beyond.

'You must know this little area better than anyone, so if

you can tell me anything about the tenants of that building before I question them . . .'

But the huge, pale stones of the palace wall were bending and lifting before the Marshal's tinted gaze as he walked. The aspirin had worn off and his temperature was soaring. Perhaps he shouldn't even have had the coffee . . .

When they got into the office he took off his hat and dark glasses and fished for a handkerchief. He was shivering and his forehead was damp.

'Good God, man, you're sick!'

'Sorry . . . I think I'll have to lie down . . .' It was all he could do to get himself through to his quarters, out of his coat and jacket and on to the bed, clutching the chemist's white package. To his surprise, Carabiniere Bacci had followed him. He was too ill and too preoccupied to interpret this unwonted attention; he was worried about the little cleaner. He swallowed two tablets and lay back.

'Tell him . . . tell him I may not get to the funeral if I'm no better.' His eyes were closed and his face red. 'But I can send a wreath . . . she was only young, you know . . . cancer, the brother-in-law said . . . and he's not as old as he looks . . . must have been murder, I suppose . . . blood soaked into the carpet . . . but not much of it . . . not much . . . Carabiniere Bacci?'

'Yes, sir?'

'What am I talking about?'

'You'd better get some rest, sir. Is there anything else you want?'

There was no answer.

So it was the Captain who sat in the Marshal's chair and questioned the cleaner while Carabiniere Bacci took notes.

Gianpaolo Maria Cipolla, born in Salerno in 1938, resident in Florence, Via Romana 83 red, since 1952, widower, arrived in Via Maggio 58 on Wednesday, December 22nd, at

his customary hour of 6 A.M., to clean the entrance hall and
stairs of the building and polish the brass plate and doorknobs outside. He had his own key to the gates of the courtyard because once a month he cleaned that too, but he had
no key to the front door. He was always able to get in because
the bank cleaners did have keys and they arrived at about
the same time. He had not seen the bank cleaners on the
morning of the 22nd but whenever they arrived first they left
the door ajar for him. He had no key to the lift, each tenant
had his own. He used the stairs and started his cleaning at
the top. He had seen, at the foot of the stairs, the door of the
ground-floor flat open and a light on. He had gone in and
seen the Englishman dead on the floor and had telephoned
for the Marshal, instead of ringing 113, the emergency number, because the Marshal lived near his sister, who was married to a gardener in the Boboli. After telephoning he had
sat down to wait.

The Captain turned to Carabiniere Bacci. 'Was the door
to the flat open or closed when you arrived?'

'Open, sir.'

'I opened it for you.' Cipolla was still terrified of address-
ing the Captain. 'I shut it when I first went in but then I
opened it for you.'

'Then why didn't you open the main doors for me, too?
There is an electronic switch inside the flat?'

'No . . . not in the ground-floor flat, only the others
upstairs.'

'Well, why didn't you come out and open the doors?'

'I was going to . . . it didn't seem right leaving him . . . a
dead man, after all . . . I was going to but then I heard you
come in . . .'

'The night guard let me in, sir.'

'Find him. I want to know if he saw anything and what

time he made his last round before that one. We'll have to call in the bank cleaners, too. It's a pity you didn't notice them this morning.'

Carabiniere Bacci blushed. He could have sworn there was no light on in the building when he arrived but he had been so nervous . . .

The Captain rose to leave them. 'Go to the British Consulate first, they may be able to tell us something, and telephone your report to me as soon as you get back here. Don't disturb the Marshal, the more rest he gets the better. I'll send him a Brigadier.'

'Right, sir.' This was the sort of person Carabiniere Bacci wanted to work for, elegant, authoritative, precise. And the Marshal out of the way in bed. Carabiniere Bacci was ecstatic.

The little cleaner still stood there after the Captain had left. 'You can go home,' Carabiniere Bacci told him. 'We'll get in touch with you if we need you, and when the case is formalized you'll have to make an official statement at the Public Prosecutor's office.'

The cleaner still looked uncertain what to do, he kept glancing at the door through which the Marshal had disappeared. Carabiniere Bacci, remembering the message, understood. 'The Marshal asked me to tell you that he might not be well enough to attend the funeral, he's got flu quite badly, but he will be sending a wreath . . . and if I may also offer my condolences . . .'

'Thank you . . . have I to go, then . . . ?' He looked vaguely about him as though he thought he had left something, his narrow shoulders a little hunched, his brush of dark hair giving him a look of permanent surprise. He crept nervously out into the cold, shivering in his thin cotton overall.

Half way up Via Maggio, on his way to the British

Consulate, Carabiniere Bacci stopped to have himself shaved. When he crossed the Santa Trinita bridge his cheeks were clean and tingling in the damp air. The morning fog, instead of lifting, had settled down, blotting out the weak sun. Upriver, the ghost of the Ponte Vecchio with its tiny windows lit was straddling nothing; downriver the swollen olive-green current, and the yellow and gray buildings flanking it, dissolved into the fog after a few hundred yards.

CHAPTER 2

BY THREE IN THE afternoon the day was fading, and Carabiniere Bacci, still in his greatcoat, switched on the light in the office before he picked up the telephone receiver. As he was about to dial he heard the Marshal calling him and he went through to the bedroom. The Marshal was still in bed and had got into his pajamas. He seemed to be breathing with difficulty.

'What time is it?'

'Just after three. Do you have to take more tablets?'

'Not till five . . . You look wet, is it raining?'

'It's started to drizzle, nothing much, but it's already going dark. I have to phone the Captain.'

'What's happening?'

'I spent most of the morning at the British Consulate with a girl called Signorina Lowry.'

'What was she like?'

'Very pretty, she has red hair—'

'Carabiniere Bacci,' breathed the Marshal, 'I'm delighted if you've fallen in love but I would like to know if she was helpful, if they're going to cooperate.'

'Yes, sir. Yes, she was very helpful, she rang the Embassy in Rome where they know him better and the Consul himself informed the family in England. The only thing is, she said the family might cause us some problems depending on what attitude they take, but we shall just have to wait and see. I went to see the night guard next, he lives over in Via Fiesolana, and when I got there I had to wait for him to get up. He insists that the door to the ground-floor flat was closed every time he passed it—'

'The shutters . . .'

'Sir?'

'You said it was going dark . . . close the shutters before you go, and switch on the light, not the big one . . . the lamp, here by me . . . that's right . . .' The Marshal's eyes were closed and there were a few drops of sweat on his forehead and nose. Carabiniere Bacci went back to the office, closing the door softly.

The Captain seemed equally determined to interrupt his report.

'—The present Consul only met him once at one of the Mayor's receptions—the previous Consul may have known him better but he's retired and before that the Englishman was at the Embassy in Rome. His registration card—'

'Yes, all right, we'll get to all that later. Your trip to the Consulate seems to have caused something of a stir; we're to be honored by a visit from two Scotland Yard men—the Englishman evidently had relatives in high places. Our visitors will be on this afternoon's flight so they should be here about four-thirty. How's your English?'

'Quite good, sir.'

'Then be in my office here in an hour. How's the Marshal?'

'Not too good, still in bed . . . there's nobody here, sir, in the office . . . I mean . . .'

'I know. At this time of year it's practically impossible but there's a man on his way so wait for him—I can't leave him there all night. Is the Marshal . . . ?'

'He needs to rest, sir. I'll be here.'

'Yes . . . you'll perhaps be good enough to telephone me if anything happens.'

'Yes, sir,' said Carabiniere Bacci meekly.

φ φ φ

'SUNNY ITALY,' remarked the Chief Inspector drily as they crossed the tarmac at Pisa, with their collars turned up against the foggy drizzle.

'It is December, sir,' the young Inspector ventured to remind him.

They were an unlikely couple. Inspector Jeffreys considered his chief to be a typical product of a third-rate public school, whose ignorance was only exceeded by his arrogance. The Chief thought Jeffreys was 'jumped-up working class with a chip on his shoulder and no proper respect.' Less prejudiced colleagues considered the Chief to have been, in his day, a good 'thief-taker,' and the younger man to be exceptionally bright. It was said he would make a name for himself if he didn't get sacked first. The story of how, during his first week on the beat, he had booked the Mayor's car three times for being parked outside his mistress's house all night without lights was likely to follow him throughout his career. The Chief Inspector had been sent out to Florence as the man who would conduct matters so as to avoid any unpleasantness for the Langley-Smythe family. Jeffreys had been sent to get him off a delicate case at home, on the excuse that he could speak a bit of Italian. During their last hurried lunch in the canteen the Chief paused in his labors with a huge wedge of pie and chips to advise: 'Tuck in, Jeffreys, this is the last decent food we're likely to see for a few days.'

On the plane Jeffreys had read a guide to Florence to avoid conversation.

A pullman coach took them from Pisa to Florence. Along the motorway the bare orchards and plowed fields on either side were shrouded in gray mist. A Carabiniere car met them

at the terminal and plunged them into the labyrinthine center of the city where the wet roofs seemed to meet overhead
and the long streets with their interminable rows of louvred
shutters got narrower and narrower, all of them, in the gray
half-light, looking the same. They got a brief glimpse of the
river embankment, then moved away again without crossing
over. Two armed guards in napoleonic hats saluted them as
an electronic gate slid open, and they were passed on to a
young lieutenant whose gleaming black cavalry boots and
dangling sword they followed up a wide staircase and along a
series of corridors. The light was on in the Captain's large
office. He rose behind his desk to greet them; Carabiniere
Bacci was already on his feet. The Englishmen introduced
themselves.

'Chief Inspector Lowestoft, New Scotland Yard, and this
is Inspector Jeffreys.'

Some brief, polite speeches were translated by the younger
men who were sizing each other up at the same time.
Inspector Jeffreys, running an eye over the immaculate front-
age of Carabiniere Bacci, pulled his crumpled mackintosh
around him and remembered he had a button missing, which
none of his three current girlfriends had been willing to sew
on for him. Carabiniere Bacci, regarding the other's loose
brown curls and casual attire, was feeling hopelessly inferior
in the face of such ebullient confidence. The Chief Inspector
was for getting down to business.

'As far as you're concerned we're here quite unofficially,
let's say to offer any assistance we can with the English side of
this business. Mr. Langley-Smythe's sister is married to . . .
well, to a man of some influence who would like to know
exactly what the situation is and to avoid unnecessary distress for his wife, which is why he wanted somebody on the
spot—we're not here to interfere in any way with your

inquiries, naturally . . .' He watched Carabiniere Bacci's face intently as he translated this, as though to prevent his making any unauthorized changes. The Captain was a little ill at ease, knowing that his English was too basic for him to converse with the Chief Inspector at first hand. The Chief was a bit put out by this deficiency of the Captain's himself, but he persevered.

'I imagine we can make ourselves useful by interviewing Mr. Langley-Smythe's English friends and so on, building up a picture of the sort of person he was—we already know, of course, that he was a gentleman of independent means and extremely well-connected. You probably know that he worked at the Embassy in Rome up until his retirement five years ago.'

'We always consider it an honor,' offered the Captain gallantly in return, 'when someone chooses to remain in our beautiful country when no longer detained by business.'

'Yes . . .' mused the Chief Inspector, on receiving a translation of this morsel of eloquence, 'I suppose so. Rum thing to do, really, but I suppose he'd got used to it by then, made friends and so on—there are quite a few English people here, are there?'

'Many. It is also marginally possible, of course, that Mr. Langley-Smythe might have made some Italian friends too.' The irony was lost in Carabiniere Bacci's translation.

'Mmm . . .' The Chief thought it more polite not to answer that one. 'He seems to have made an enemy, at any rate.'

'Unless the motive was an entirely impersonal one, that of robbery.'

'No, no. I wouldn't think so. Armed robbery means professional robbery and something worth stealing. Mr. Langley-Smythe was comfortably off, of course, but nothing spectacular, and what money he had was invested in England. According to his bank, he drew out a very modest amount each month, presumably for his living expenses. He wasn't a great spender or a collector either so it doesn't seem—was there anything stolen?'

'No. Nothing stolen, as far as we know.'

'Well, then . . . ?' The Chief Inspector looked at Carabiniere Bacci for an explanation, then at the Captain who was looking down at his own hands on the desk.

'Nothing was stolen, Chief Inspector, but there was a great deal that might have been. My men found a safe in the bedroom wall, open, containing, in various currencies, a little less than half a million pounds sterling. He would also seem to have had other investments than his English ones. According to his lawyer here in Florence, he had considerable investments in this country and a numbered account in a Zurich bank. Possibly your . . . gentleman of influence did not feel able to be entirely frank with you in this respect.'

Carabiniere Bacci's embarrassment over the translation of this speech was greatly increased by his conviction that he had just seen one of Inspector Jeffreys's bright blue eyes wink at him.

'Not at all, not at all.' The Chief was red-faced. 'Of course, there was no time to discuss these things at any length. We had a report of a murder, not a robbery.'

'Quite. However, the possibility remains that there might have been an attempt at robbery, perhaps disturbed by the victim. Shall we come to the cause of death . . .'

Inspector Jeffreys gazed out of the tall window at the lights in the building opposite. He could hear a lot of traffic going by in the wet and the occasional police car leaving with its siren going. His Italian had more or less given out after the polite preliminaries, and he had no interest in this case if they were only here to do a whitewash job. Bloke was probably queer, the foreign service was full of them. He followed the Captain's words spasmodically.

'. . . 6.35. One shot, fairly close range from behind. The bullet pierced the left ventricle and death was virtually instantaneous. He had been dead for some hours, when we find out where and when he ate we can be more accurate, but Professor Forli tells me that death probably occurred during the early hours of the morning.'

'The weapon?'

'My men are still looking for it. A large number of different fingerprints were found in the living-room of the flat, so we must assume, since he lived alone and employed no domestic staff, that he received a great many visitors. We're checking the prints with our files at the moment. That's really as much as I can tell you at this stage, except that he was found by the stair cleaner in the early morning, and—'

The telephone rang.

'Gianini here, sir, technical squad. I've got the information you wanted on that majolica bust. Doctor Biondini recognized the piece immediately, said he checked that seal himself only six months ago. The head of an angel by Delia Robbia, Luca, not Andrea. It's a particularly good piece, he said.'

'I see. Well, this throws new light on our man.'

'More than you'd think, sir.'

'Meaning . . . ?'

'I said that Biondini checked that seal only six months ago. He wanted to check his files to make absolutely sure, in the circumstances, that he couldn't be mistaken.'

'And?'

'He wasn't mistaken. The Delia Robbia belongs to an American woman who has a villa up near Fiesole. She married into an impoverished family of Italian nobility before the war, and with his knowledge and her money they started collecting. The husband died about six years ago.'

'And she sold the piece?'

'No. She didn't. It couldn't have been sold, Biondini says, without his knowledge. Besides which, she's been in California for the past two months, visiting relatives there, leaving only the servants, a married couple, in the house.'

'And are they still there?'

'No reply, sir. Biondini's on his way up there now.'

'I'll send somebody—but he'll have to get on to the Protection of Patrimony group; I can't deal with it—tell him I'd like to be kept informed. Yes. Yes. Thank you.' The Captain replaced the receiver and remained silent for some moments. He didn't relish the idea of announcing to the Chief Inspector that his respectable compatriot was now suspected of being a thief, or, at least, a receiver. There was no possibility of his having bought the piece legitimately since it was registered and could not be sold, or even moved, without the approval of the State. He tried an oblique approach:

'You don't happen to know whether Mr. Langley-Smythe had an English gun licence?'

'I could check on it for you. Why? Did he have an Italian one?'

'No, he didn't. But he might have had a weapon, nevertheless . . .'

'Has such a weapon been found? Is there any evidence to suggest he had a gun?'

'No, not as yet . . .'

'Well, if you don't mind my saying so, it seems to me that you're trying to make a case against Mr. Langley-Smythe instead of against whoever killed him.' The Chief's pale blue eyes were suddenly bright. Jeffreys knew what that meant and was listening now, watching the Captain's face as an embarrassed Carabiniere Bacci translated. The Captain showed no sign of anger but he became even more formal and excessively polite.

'I am very sorry indeed that you should think so. However, I'm sure you realize, from your own extensive experience in such a renowned place as Scotland Yard, that I am obliged to consider all possibilities, including those which are as unwelcome to me as they are to you.'

Smoothy, thought Jeffreys, impressed.

'Yes, well, Mr. Langley-Smythe didn't shoot himself.'

'Indeed not. But we both know that no professional would use a 6.35 or aim at the heart. It is, on the other hand, the sort of weapon often kept for self-defence, which makes it possible that a thief might have found it on the spot and made use of it if he had been disturbed.'

'Well, naturally, I'd thought of that. It's just a question of attitude . . .'

But the situation was defused. The cold glint in the Chief's eye, normally reserved for picket lines and left-wing militants, was fading. 'Will there be any objection to our removing the body to England for burial?'

'I imagine not. At the moment it's in the Medico-Legal Institute at Careggi. The British Consulate will deal with all the formalities and once Professor Forli has completed his autopsy you can apply to the Substitute Prosecutor for permission.' The business of the stolen bust would have to wait. It would have been easier if there had been just the two of them but with the language problem . . .

'Well, that's really as much as I can tell you at this stage. If you wouldn't mind'—he looked at his watch—'I'd like to get back to Via Maggio now and start interviewing the tenants. If we can offer you any assistance with accommodation?'

'No need, thanks all the same. Nice girl from the Consulate fixed us up at the English vicarage—convenient enough—it's on the same street as the scene of the crime, she was telling us; we haven't been there yet. Hotels all seemed to be full up. Funny thing at this time of year.'

'Christmas shoppers, Chief Inspector. Florence is a renowned shopping center for the whole world, as is your own city.'

'I suppose so. Well, we'll get along to the vicarage. We may as well make a start by having a chat to the vicar. No doubt Mr. Langley-Smythe was a churchgoer.'

'No doubt. I'll order a car for you.' He picked up his internal phone and rang a bell for the escort. 'Might I suggest that we meet here tomorrow? Late morning would be best, perhaps; I should have a full autopsy report by then, and possibly something from Records on the prints . . . shall we say eleven-thirty?'

'Right. That'll give us time to make a few inquiries among the English community—with your permission, of course.'

'By all means. I should be grateful. And if you would then be my guests for lunch?'

'WELL, THAT went off all right,' said the Chief Inspector, settling into the back of the car. Jeffreys didn't trust himself to speak.

It was quite dark by now and still raining softly through the mist. As they crossed the river they got a glimpse of soft haloes of pink and yellow light around the miniature shops on the Ponte Vecchio in the distance, and the faint glimmer of what must have been a huge civic Christmas tree somewhere higher up. Their route took them by a complicated one-way system through the popular quarter where the streets, crowded with people, seemed too narrow for the car. The shops were at their busiest at this time of the evening and their wares overflowed on to the pavement. Shoppers milled about in the road, their umbrellas glistening in the dark. Tinsel glittered even in the windows of grocers' shops which were hung with Tuscan hams and fat sausages. Pyramids of tangerines were interspersed with shining leaves. Their driver was continually sounding his horn and they moved at a snail's pace.

'Wouldn't fancy being a bus driver round here,' remarked the Chief. Jeffreys only grunted, his eyes fixed on all the food that was passing his hungry gaze.

Via Maggio, although busy, was more sedate. Only an occasional poinsettia standing in a copper bowl in front of the dark velvets and inlaid woods of the antique-dealers' windows gave any indication of the season. At the river end of the street they stopped in front of a fifteenth-century palace that housed the English church on the ground floor and the vicar's apartment on the first.

Inspector Jeffreys paused to thank the Carabiniere driver in careful Italian. The driver was pleased.

'If you go out and get lost,' he offered, evidently considering this a likely possibility, 'find the river and the Santa Trinita bridge—there it is, with a statue at each corner, one for each of the four seasons, you can't miss it—then you're home.'

'Thanks.'

'It's nothing. See you again.' He drove off across the bridge toward the blurred lights of the city center.

The vicar was on the doorstep, rubbing his hands.

'Come in, come in,' he said, clasping each of their hands

in turn, 'Felicity's just making a cup of tea. What a miserable evening!'

THE CAPTAIN arrived in Via Maggio with Carabiniere Bacci still in attendance. As they passed the deserted porter's lodge of number fifty-eight he indicated the boarded-up window: 'At one time we could have done most of our inquiring right here—and in a *palazzo signorile* like this one it matters more than ever. You can be sure that these tenants hardly speak to each other and that none of them even know what's happened in the building despite the fact that one of my men has been standing guard on the ground floor all day.'

They had brought another guard to relieve the first. 'I'll send someone else toward eleven o'clock . . .'

They walked up to the first floor where R. Cesarini, Antiquario, was the only tenant, and Carabiniere Bacci rang the bell. They waited in silence beside a thick fragment of Roman pillar with a huge potted plant standing on it next to the lift. The fluted wooden doors of the flat had two heavy iron knockers cast in the shape of heads. They heard rapid, shuffling footsteps and bolts being quietly drawn. A young Eritrean woman opened one door cautiously and peered round it. She wore a blue nylon overall but her head was shrouded in a traditional white muslin veil.

'Polizia . . . ?' she asked wonderingly.

'Carabinieri. We'd like to speak to Signor Cesarini.'

'In shop.' She pointed vaguely. Behind her a glossy pale marble floor stretched deep into the background. A warm light was shining behind double stained-glass doors on the left, making colored patterns on a carved oak chest that stood in the hall.

'He has two shops further up Via Maggio, sir,' murmured Carabiniere Bacci.

The Captain looked at his watch: six . . . the shop would hardly close before eight. They could go round there after questioning the other tenants. 'We'd like a word with you, in the meantime,' he told the maid.

She let them into the hall reluctantly, but she could tell them nothing. She had heard no strange or sudden noises in the night. She had seen no one unusual in the building. She didn't know the Englishman. She seemed astonished that they should expect her to know what went on in the building, as if her limited Italian prevented her from seeing or hearing anything outside her own door. She continually clutched with thin fingers at her veil as if she would have liked to hide behind it; the gesture, coupled with her small stature, gave the impression of an old woman, though she must have been in her early twenties. Her big dark eyes kept straying worriedly to the end of the passage behind her. Probably she should have been preparing the supper.

'Is your employer married?'

'Yes. Married.'

'And his wife? Where is she?'

'Go to Calabria . . . and the children. Christmas. There is family . . .'

'And Signor Cesarini?'

'He will go in two days.'

'And you?'

'Me?'

'Where will you go for Christmas, Signorina?'

'Here.'

'Alone?' The Captain glanced involuntarily beyond her at the vast apartment in which she, no doubt, had one tiny bedroom. 'Do you have any friends in Florence?'

'Friends, yes. Eritrean friends. Girls like me.'

'I see. Thank you. We'll speak to Signor Cesarini in his shop.'

'Something is wrong?'

'No.' He realized at once she was thinking of her job, her papers. 'Nothing wrong as far as you're concerned. A man on the ground floor was killed last night and we need to know if anyone heard anything or saw any strangers in the building, that's all. We needn't disturb you any longer.'

She showed no reaction to the news. After closing the door behind them they heard her rapid steps shuffle away on the marble floor toward the kitchen.

The second floor was divided into two flats. From behind the door on the left came the halting notes of Schubert's 'Serenade' played on the piano. From the right, someone practising an aria from *Rigoletto*. Carabiniere Bacci looked at the Captain.

'Schubert first, I think.' As they waited, after ringing the bell, he said, 'You're a Florentine?' remembering the information about Cesarini's shop.

'Yes, sir.' Carabiniere Bacci blushed with pleasure at being noticed.

'Back in school after Christmas?'

'Yes, sir.' He would have liked to say more but the Captain's seriousness, his gravity, was like a barrier around him. It was impossible even to imagine him smiling. 'Should I ring again, sir?'

But the door marked Cipriani was opening. Another marble entrance hall with Persian carpets, a Venetian glass chandelier, a stiff, brocaded chair with two schoolbags thrown on it. Only as their gazes drifted downward did they see who had opened the door: a small, fat girl with shiny black short hair and enormous round eyes. She wore a white school pinafore with its blue satin bow twisted up under one ear and she was staring up at them with disconcerting fervor.

'Are your parents at home?'

Without taking her eyes from them for a second, she opened her mouth until the rest of her face almost vanished and, drowning the warbling tenor next door and the piano behind her, she bellowed: 'Ma-ma!' and fled.

The Schubert continued, limping a little at the difficult bits. The tenor next door sang on. No one else appeared.

'Shall I . . . ?'

'You'd better. Ring two or three times.'

Still they were left waiting by the open door. They noticed a metronome clicking along with the piano. Some harassed voices were heard in the distance.

'But, Signora, what am I to do? I can't leave this sauce!'

A muffled reply, then:

'She's already been and says they're big black men! I think she's left the door open!'

'Mamma!' Small running feet.

'I'm coming . . . wait . . .'

At the end of the marble passage a blurred white figure appeared behind an 'art-deco' glass panel. A woman in a white, hooded bathrobe came out. The dark head of the child reappeared round a side door: 'You see!' She ran off, giggling uncontrollably.

The woman came toward them, clopping on high-heeled slippers. Her skin was still rosy and damp from the bath and she was blotting her wet hair with the embroidered towelling hood.

'What's happened? What's the matter—not an accident! Vincenzo—'

'No, Signora, please don't distress yourself. We're making routine inquiries.'

'Oh, of course, the robbery.'

'Robbery?'

'Wasn't the bank downstairs robbed again? My maid said there was a policeman down there when she did the shopping—we're having a lot of people to supper, my husband's family—his niece is getting engaged and so . . . oh dear . . . you'd better come in. I hope you'll excuse me, I've just taken a bath . . . come inside . . ."

'Signora!'

'I'm coming! Oh, heavens—if you could just wait *one* moment I could explain to her . . .'

'Yes, of course.'

She hurried away and they waited in the hall by the open door on the right through which the child had vanished. There was what seemed to be a playroom there, a speckled marble floor with a red, long-haired rug, a child's tricycle, books, a row of dolls on a sofa, an open door leading into a smaller room beyond. There, the struggling pianist was partly visible, her white tunic moving stiffly in time to the metronome. Every so often the music stopped and there was some animated whispering. Then it would continue.

The woman returned. She seemed to wonder which would be the right room in which to receive them. She had tied the bathrobe around her more carefully. Eventually her distracted gaze settled on the playroom: 'In here, if you'd like to . . .'

They sat down among the toys, holding their hats.

'I'm afraid I don't know anything about the robbery except what my maid—'

'There hasn't been a robbery, Signora.'

'But—'

'There's been a murder.'

The color quickly left her face. 'Here . . . ?'

'The ground floor. Your neighbor, Mr. Langley-Smythe.'

'Oh . . . the Englishman.'

'You knew him?'

'By sight, of course. I knew he was English. He always said "Good day, Signora" in that funny flat way that English people . . . and so he's dead . . . ?'

'He was shot. Probably in the early hours of this morning; we're trying to fix the exact time. We'd like you to think back and try and remember if you might have heard any sudden noise in the night—or even if you woke suddenly without knowing what woke you—there was only one shot.'

'No, nothing. Nothing would wake me, you see, because I always take a sleeping pill, so . . .'

'Perhaps the children? If you could call them and ask them yourself—no need to say what's happened—whether they heard any strange noises during the night or saw anyone unfamiliar in the building at any time recently. The maid, too, if she sleeps here.'

'No, she doesn't; she comes in at eight to take the children to school and she usually leaves at six—it's just that today with this supper—'

'Yes, you have guests. The children, then . . .'

The two little girls were brought in. The small fat one had stopped giggling and taken to staring again. The young pianist, a slim, solemn girl, dark-haired like her sister, was also wearing a white school pinafore, but with the blue satin neck bow neatly in place. They stood side by side in silence.

'Children, these gentlemen are Carabinieri and they have to ask you some questions. There's nothing to be afraid of; they just want to know if either of you heard any strange noises in the night . . . anything that woke you up . . .'

No reaction from the two solemn faces. Eventually the older one said, 'No, Mamma, I didn't hear anything.'

They all looked at the little one. Her fat cheeks were getting steadily redder as she suppressed a giggle. Her mother tugged the satin bow round to the front of the white collar and smoothed it.

'Come on, now, Giovanna, it's very important for them to know if you heard something.'

The big eyes flashed from her mother to the two men and back again. She looked about to pop. Then she took a sudden, deep breath and opened her mouth.

'Bang!'

And before they could interrupt her she had heaved another great breath:

'Bang!'

She beamed upon the assembled company and added, 'That's what I heard, Mamma.'

CHAPTER 3

'Speaking . . . Professor . . . you've been very quick . . .'

'Doesn't take long, and I was working on him when you phoned, so . . .'

'And the results?'

'Negative.'

'Negative? You're absolutely sure?'

'Are you doubting my—'

'No! No, nothing like that. It's just that we now have a witness, only a child, admittedly, who swears there were two shots . . . it seemed to be the only possibility—that the Englishman had fired first, the gun being his, and managed to wound his attacker since there's no trace of any other bullet in the room . . .'

'Or of any other blood.'

'No, I realize that. Even so, it's a possibility.'

'Remember, this one was shot in the back.'

'I realize that, too; he'd hardly have turned his back in such circumstances but the child insists on the two bangs and I must confess that I think she's telling the truth. I can't ignore it because it doesn't fit some preconceived idea . . .'

'That's true, but I'm afraid I can't help you. The Englishman has not fired a gun, there isn't a trace. I can give you a rough report on my other findings, if you . . .'

'No—unless there's anything startling—I mustn't keep these people and I still have the rest of the tenants to see. If you could get something to me by about eleven tomorrow . . .'

'Easily.'

'Thank you. I'm sorry I had to disturb you.'

'You didn't. I shall probably be here till nine. We're short-staffed, of course.'

'Of course. Till tomorrow then . . .'

The Ciprianis' dinner guests had been shown into the drawing-room across the passage from the playroom and were whispering and murmuring there. The Signora had gone off to dress. When the Captain returned to the play-room, the father, not long returned and still with his heavy, rainspotted overcoat slung round his shoulders, was on his knees pleading with little Giovanna who, with a gleam in her eye, had refused to elucidate unless she could sit on Carabiniere Bacci's knee. Carabiniere Bacci, distressed and deeply embarrassed, sat very still and stiff, as though he were holding a bundle of dynamite. The child was now wearing his hat and had twice been deterred from taking possession of his automatic. Schubert had started up again in the next room.

'But, Giovanna, my little bean, my little treasure,' pleaded Signor Cipriani, 'these gentlemen are quite sure . . .'

But Little Treasure was adamant. Bang. Then another bang. Two bangs.

'Close together?' asked the Captain suddenly, thinking that perhaps an echo . . . in a building that size with its great stairwell . . .

Giovanna pondered this point solemnly under her big hat before saying, 'No. A long time apart.' She wriggled herself round to address Carabiniere Bacci: 'Let me play with your gun—for one minute?'

'No,' said Carabiniere Bacci stiffly. 'Little girls don't like guns. Wouldn't you like to get down?'

'No. Little girls do like guns—I've got two of them and

one's pink and shoots water but I've lost it and I'm getting a bow and arrow as well from the Befana and a—'

'Giovanna! If you don't behave the Befana will bring you a piece of coal for Epiphany, never mind a bow and arrow, now you—'

'No!'

'What do you mean, no?'

'The Befana's a good witch, Granny said so. She might bring me some coal as well as a bow and arrow, sugar coal from the shop!'

'Giovanna, Giovanna! This is very serious! Now, please listen to the Captain . . .'

The doorbell rang and the maid passed by on her way to answer it. They heard her pick up the housephone and ask, 'Who is it?' before pressing the electronic switch for the main door of the building.

There came an echoing boom from below as the visitors closed the great doors behind them.

'There,' said Giovanna, pleased to have her point so conveniently proved, 'Bang.'

The Captain and Carabiniere Bacci closed their eyes in quiet exasperation.

'You heard the big door close?' the Captain began again patiently. 'I expect it was somebody visiting. And then you heard the door again when they left. Perhaps it wasn't so late as you think and the second bang was just someone going away.'

'No. Nobody went away. The door only banged once. The second bang was a big bang.'

'And it wasn't the door?'

'No.' After a pause she added reluctantly, looking away sideways, 'A gun bang.'

'Why do you think it was a gun bang?'

The child made no answer but went on looking away.

'Like something you heard on television, was it?'

She took off the hat and looked down at it in silence.

'Is it something you saw? Something that frightened you?'

'I want to get down.' She slid off Carabiniere Bacci's knee.

'Do you think you're absolutely sure about the time? The time of the first bang?' The Captain turned to Signor Cipriani questioningly.

'Yes, she can tell the time, she's a very bright child, you know. She has a little clock by her bed.'

'With Mickey Mouse on it.'

'And it was a quarter to three?'

'Yes.' She gave Carabiniere Bacci his hat back. 'Papa, I want to go.' The Captain nodded his permission to the father, who released Giovanna. They watched her slip quickly out of the room. Almost immediately there was a noise of pattering and shuffling followed by a gleeful squeal.

'Strange,' murmured the Captain, 'I would have said she was hiding something, possibly out of fear, but she seems cheerful enough now.' They heard more shuffling steps and a voice calling out:

'Giovanna! How often must I tell you not to slide along the passage! It's dangerous . . . Vincenzo!' The Signora reappeared in the doorway, seeking her husband. She was dressed, elegantly dressed, but with a touch of bewildered dishevelment that might have to do with the dinner-party or be habitual but which was certainly attractive.

'I beg your pardon, Signora, for our still being here, but I must ask you if we might take a look into the little girls' bedroom, to check whether she could have seen anything at all . . .'

'Vincenzo . . . ?'

'Why don't you give everyone an aperitif? I'll see to this.'

He took them to the bedroom which the two little girls shared. One bed, against the wall, was immaculate, its snowy quilt smooth. The other, under the window, was in chaos, the crumpled quilt trailing on the floor, the pages of a comic scattered around it. The father was embarrassed:

'Children, these days, you know . . .'

They looked out of the window. Unless the Englishman had been shot in the center of the courtyard and then brought back in, the child could have seen nothing. Her bedroom window was directly above that of the ground-floor flat. They turned away. Something black was sticking out under Giovanna's pillow; a plastic revolver. 'There's nothing to be done with her,' shrugged the distracted father, 'it's her passion.'

'Well,' the Captain pointed out, 'she's been a great help to us in fixing the time of death. We're grateful for that.'

'Yes, she's a very light sleeper, in fact. I've known her call out to me when I've come home well after midnight . . .' He blushed faintly.

The Captain, whose tolerance normally almost amounted to indifference, could not have said exactly why that faint blush made him angry.

'Might I ask your occupation, Signor Cipriani?'

'Certainly. I'm an insurance broker; my offices are in the Piazza della Republica.'

'And did you arrive home after midnight last night?'

'I believe it was about one o'clock . . .' He blushed again, sensing the Captain's hostility. 'I dined with some clients at Doney's.'

'You realize that we'll have to check that? And the time you left?'

'You mean I'm a suspect?'

'I mean that I must know where every tenant was after

midnight last night. Was your wife awake when you got home?'

'I think so . . . yes, she was reading a book.'

The Captain's inexplicable anger subsided as quickly as it had risen. 'Do you know anything about your neighbor, Mr. Langley-Smythe?'

'Nothing, really, except that he was English.'

'You didn't notice whether he had many visitors?'

'Visitors? I never saw any. He seemed a solitary sort of man . . . Of course, he could have had, without my ever seeing them.'

'But if he'd had an exceptional number of visitors, frequently that is, you'd probably have noticed?'

'Perhaps . . . but in a building this size . . . and I'm out a great deal. I wouldn't care to say anything definite . . .'

'I see. What about the other tenants? Do you know much about them?'

'Not a great deal—oh, except that the Frediani upstairs are away—the wife is American, he's a jeweler on the Ponte Vecchio—they left yesterday, I met them when I was leaving in the morning. They were getting into a taxi with a lot of luggage. They wished me a happy Christmas—apparently they're spending theirs in America with her family.'

'Do you know where in America?'

'I'm afraid I don't . . . you could ask their neighbor, Miss White, she may know. It's possible she may know the wife as they're both English-speaking.'

'Signorina White doesn't go away for Christmas?'

'I don't think so, I think she's still here.'

'Thank you. We'll try her . . . And what about your neighbor on this floor?'

'The Judge?' They were making their way back to the front door. 'He's at home, as you can hear. He's retired and lives alone except for his housekeeper. I'm afraid I don't know much about him other than that he's fond of Verdi.'

'Well, thank you, anyway, you've been very helpful . . .' An exaggeration, but the Captain was ashamed of his momentary loss of temper, which he felt to be a loss of dignity. 'Without a resident porter our job is very difficult.'

'Ah, Captain—' Signor Cipriani opened his hands in despair—'you know how much a porter costs, these days? At least six million a year . . . and that's if you can find anybody to do it. Even with the present housing shortage, young people today wouldn't consider it. Well, we're always here, if there's anything else you want to ask . . .'

The Judge could tell them nothing. Both he and his housekeeper had been in the house all night and had not been disturbed by any noise. The housekeeper confessed to taking sleeping pills and the Judge said he was a heavy sleeper and nothing ever woke him. They both retired early. They only knew the Englishman by sight, a nodding acquaintance. To the best of their knowledge he had never had any visitors.

They had been received in an austere, book-lined room that looked as though it were never used. The Judge himself was a tall, dry-looking man, severe, almost morose. It didn't seem possible that he could be the owner of the robust voice they had heard from outside. Nevertheless, when they found themselves once again on the broad stone staircase the voice was warbling *Bella figlia del amore* with as much sweetness and passion as ever. They began the climb to the top floor.

Miss White's door was wide open.

'Don't be frightened! Come in!' a voice instructed them loudly in English. Its owner remained invisible. The two men looked at each other.

'She's telling us to come in,' explained Carabiniere Bacci, mystified. 'Perhaps she's heard that we're here.'

Hesitantly, they took off their hats and stepped into the entrance hall of polished terracotta tiles.

'Carry on, carry on! I'll be with you in a minute. No charge! Ha ha!'

The Captain looked at Carabiniere Bacci for an explanation.

'I'm not sure what . . .'

They moved further in and looked about them. There was an oil painting hung in the hall of a pink-faced old man with snowy hair and beard. A brass plate below informed them: 'Walter Savage Landor, Poet, born Warwick 1775, died Florence 1864.' They were looking at the painting when a head popped suddenly out at them from a doorway next to it. A small lady in her mid-sixties, smartly dressed but wearing running shoes, leaped forward, beaming.

'Carabinieri!' she squealed, delighted. 'Never had one of you before! Judge came up once, of course, but that's not the same thing, being neighbors, nice of him to come, all the same—I always think it's nice when the Italians take an interest, had everything translated and they do come—school parties, and so on, but not Carabinieri, ha ha! You're the first! Delighted to see you, I'm Miss White, curator—not really a curator, I mean I *live* here—did it all myself. If you want anything done, as they say, and keep away from committees, *I* say, lot of old bores—what's the matter with you?' She suddenly peered into Carabiniere Bacci's stunned face.

'I—I . . .'

'Well, for goodness' sake come in, no point in standing out in the entrance hall, nothing to see, ought to have a chair or two out here, I suppose, but then everybody'd think they were *his* chairs and I'd have to keep explaining—have *got* one or two things that *were* his but you can't have every-thing and it's all my own money—came over here for a holi-day and fifteen years later here I still am, ha ha! Carabinieri! You'd better sign my visitors' book. A judge is very nice of course but not the same thing, being a neighbor, if you see what I mean and then no uniform. I do like a uniform, don't you? Well, of course you do, that's obvious or you wouldn't be wearing one, stupid of me—and do you admire Landor?' She glared brightly at the Captain who opened his mouth, then shut it and looked to Carabiniere Bacci for some sort of translation.

'Bet you don't know what to say! I never do. My English mistress at school used to say never say "nice," so I never do! "Nice" is what you say about puddings, not poetry, is what she used to say and I bet this young man agrees!' She patted Carabiniere Bacci's elbow. 'He looks intelligent and *goodness* he's tall—well, you both are. D'you read a lot of peotry? I suppose you do or you wouldn't have come, ha ha! Well, I'll take you round. I've had everything translated, of course, because I do think it's nice when the Italians take an inter-est—I don't speak a word, of course, not a word, but I like to take people round myself if I can—now, *through here*, I'll speak up—*through here* it's mostly manuscripts and copies of manuscripts where I haven't got the real thing. I've had some of them framed on the walls, cheaper than buying cases, I've got some cases, of course, very good cabinetmaker, Signor Lorenzini, marvelous man, he made all these. Now, you'll recognize this poem, I should think, if you can make out the handwriting . . .'

'*For the love of God* . . .' threatened the Captain in Carabiniere Bacci's ear.

'I'm sorry, sir, I can't understand what she's saying . . .'

'Never mind what she's saying, just stop her and tell her—'

'Now then! I can't explain things to you if you're going to chat amongst yourselves—here you are, sign the book, go on, don't be frightened, you can write something in Italian. *Carabinieri!* This is really *nice!*'

Fifteen minutes later the two men were out on the landing, their heads ringing with incomprehensible information. Carabiniere Bacci was sweating with embarrassment. The Captain was white with annoyance.

'I thought you said your English was good?'

'I'm sorry, sir, I just couldn't cope . . .' He had tried repeatedly to interject the purpose of their visit but his carefully constructed sentences elicited nothing more than: 'Speak a bit of English, do you? Well done. Of course, you're only a boy. I think everyone should learn a language as young as possible—my French mistress at school used to say . . .'

He had also tried in Italian, they both had, but even the Captain's stern effort had produced nothing more than, *Si si! Si si!*' She had had everything translated, of course, nice when the Italians took an interest, but after fifteen years in the country couldn't speak a word, didn't know why but there it was—too old to start, that was it, have to start young, not a word—well '*si*,' of course, that was one word, and '*no*' was another, but that wasn't much, after fifteen years—and she'd only come out here for a holiday . . . *Carabinieri!*

They went down the stairs in silence. The guard on the ground floor saluted.

"AND THEN what?' Marshal Guarnaccia was sitting up in bed, his fever somewhat abated. The little lamp was still lit and beside it, on the bedside cupboard, was a bowl with the remains of a light clear broth in the bottom of it, brought round by Signora Bellini, the gardener's wife, sister of the little cleaner who had found the body.

'The Captain went to interview Cesarini, the antique-dealer in his shop.'

'And you're sent home in disgrace, is that it?'

'The Captain wanted me to get something to eat, have a rest . . .' But Carabiniere Bacci was mortified, his exhausted face drawn and pale.

'And did you get something to eat?'

'I went in the meat-roaster's shop in the piazza and got a hot beef sandwich and a glass of wine.'

The Marshal could imagine him, unaccustomed as he was to such proletarian living, sitting delicately on a high stool at the counter in front of the rows of hissing, crackling chickens turning on the great wood fire, trying not to get a spot on his uniform and to evade the familiar jokes of the cheerful Neapolitan in his greasy apron.

'You should have gone to the Mensa—and I hope you're not thinking of sleeping downstairs in the office again?'

'I told the Captain I would, in case the phone rings in the night. You're not fit and he can't spare anybody. The Brigadier he sent is going off now.'

'You can't expect a corpse on your doorstep every night, damn it! I'm not all that bad, as a matter of fact—I feel a bit better for that drop of soup. The fever seems to come on for a few hours at a time and then go away for a few hours. As long as I'm all right to get that train tomorrow . . .' He was gazing across the room at a photograph that stood in the shadows on a marble-topped dressing-table; two plump little boys with eyes almost as large as his own. The Marshal's passion in life was his family, his ambition to get a posting at home in Syracuse. His wife couldn't leave his mother down there alone or move her to a strange city at her age . . . He sighed and leaned back on his pillows. 'Carabiniere Bacci . . .'

'Yes, sir?'

'You're a young fool.' He pondered on this fact for a moment in silence. 'But, nevertheless . . . you've got brains . . .'

Not knowing what to say to this, Carabiniere Bacci said nothing. The Marshal pondered at such length, with his eyes closed now, that Carabiniere Bacci thought he must have fallen asleep again, but he waited. After a while the big eyes opened:

'The Captain is a serious man, a thorough man; he'll do his job. He's also, in many ways, an ambitious man, but his ambitions lie in other directions than yours—they don't include any desire to be a famous detective. You needn't blush for yourself, Carabiniere Bacci, I'm not laughing at you this time. I'm just trying to warn you that, while he will do his job conscientiously, he will want to do it so as not to upset anybody unnecessarily, not his superiors and not these Scotland Yard men. He especially won't want to cut a bad figure in front of them because that would upset both his superiors and himself, understand?'

'I think so, sir.'

'Bear it in mind, then. You have a tendency to get excited, curb it. If you rushed out and found your murderer in the next ten minutes but did it in such a way as to cause a scandal and upset those Englishmen, the Captain would not thank you. He will move carefully and you had better follow him quietly and don't get any fancy ideas.'

'No, sir.'

'I'm only trying to save you from yourself, to tell you not to stick your neck out. The Captain will wait and see which way the wind blows and you will wait and see which way *he* blows. These things are beyond you, Carabiniere Bacci.'

'Yes, sir.'

'That's because you're a Florentine. These are things that

any Sicilian over the age of five knows by experience. The Captain will do the best job he can, he's an honest man, a good man. But you would do well not to annoy him. As far as this business with the Englishwoman is concerned, I don't think you need worry too much. He'll get over that, since no one else was there to see it—and, if I know him, he'll turn it to his advantage by offering the job of questioning her to the Scotland Yard men as a gesture of friendly cooperation.'

Carabiniere Bacci's tense face relaxed a little.

'Now get out. I might as well get some rest while the fever's off me, if you won't go up to bed.'

'Right, sir. Is there anything you want?'

'No—but, Carabiniere Bacci?'

'Yes, sir?' He was opening the door.

The Marshal's eyes were closed, or seemed to be.

'If, by any chance, you should be inundated with corpses during the night, you will let me know?'

'Yes, sir.' He closed the door quietly.

The Marshal heaved a long and weary sigh, his gaze fixed on the photograph. I'll be on that train tomorrow, he thought to himself, corpses or no corpses. And he fell asleep.

It was a feverish sleep, restless, enervating, full of dreams in which he was always trying to get home, but each time having to turn back for something; he had no train ticket, he had left his station unlocked and unguarded, he had forgotten the children's presents, the bottles of water, his clothes—once he reached the platform where the train was waiting only to find that he was in his pajamas. And each time he turned back he had to struggle against such devastating heat that it left him exhausted and nauseous. Toward two in the morning he awoke, or half awoke, shivering and damp with sweat, and rolled weakly out of bed to wash and change himself. He wasn't going to be fit to travel . . . maybe Friday . . .

There were no corpses that night. Florence slept its respectable bourgeois sleep behind its tightly closed brown shutters, beneath its wet and foggy blanket, closed in the deep valley of the Arno, with a nightguard of cypress-topped hills. The cathedral bell sounded the hours from its white marble tower, echoed tinnily by out-of-tune little church bells in every quarter. But no angry telephone bell broke the exhausted sleep of Carabiniere Bacci on his camp bed. His white gloves lay undisturbed in their circle of pink light

Part Two

☙

CHAPTER 1

'WELL, THIS IS VERY nice indeed. We didn't expect this, did we, Jeffreys?'

'No, sir.'

The vicar beamed upon them: 'Felicity and I always like to have an English breakfast—it's a mystery to me how the Italians get through a morning with just a coffee and a bun. Of course, they eat much later than we do in the evening— we hear knives and forks going well after ten o'clock in some of the flats across the courtyard—so perhaps they're not so hungry in the mornings . . . but I must say, some of these people work very late . . . Felicity and I usually eat about seven, I hope that's all right with you?'

'Oh yes, I should think so.' The Chief Inspector leaned back in his chair, feeling replete after bacon and eggs, toast and marmalade and three cups of tea from a heavy silver pot. The mahogany sideboard was decked with holly and Christmas cards from England, the sort with robins, skating scenes and simple, one-color lino cuts supposed to suggest the Nativity.

'Well, I think I've just time for a pipe before I go over to the Consulate, then I must leave you boys to it.' The vicar's hair and beard were white, his face generally rather pink. He wore a hand-knitted gray sweater over his dog collar, and he sucked questioningly on his pipe as though it might tell him something. Felicity, oblivious of the two policemen, was deep in a newspaper crossword puzzle. They caught the occasional glimpse of her wispy gray hair.

'Funny sort of chappie . . .' As he struck a match and sucked a little harder, the vicar's thoughts rambled naturally to A. Langley-Smythe. 'Came to church once or twice when he first moved up here, about five years ago, I suppose, but then he stopped coming . . . didn't mix much, really.'

'Is there much social life—among the English community, that is?'

'Oh yes, yes, I think so. We do quite a lot here, you know. Felicity's awfully good—' Felicity showed no sign of life behind her newspaper—'glass of wine after the last service on Sundays, of course, and then once a month we have a little get-together—a meal, and so on—everyone makes a little something, sausage rolls, sandwiches, cakes, that sort of thing. Then at Christmas and Easter we do a hot meal and everyone contributes something to the festive board. Quite a lot of social life, really . . . The trouble is, of course, that it's the same people who give every time and others just come along . . . I'm afraid Mr. Langley-Smythe . . . well, he was a bachelor . . . couldn't expect him to bake cakes . . . but I'm afraid he didn't mix much on the few occasions when he turned up.'

'Did he have any friends, that you know of?'

'Not that I know of, do you, Felicity? No, I don't think so. Used to see him in the street every so often, but never with anyone that I can think of. He used to . . . well, he never seemed . . .'

'Never seemed what?'

'Well . . . looked after . . . bit messy, you know . . . Of course, he was a bachelor, so I suppose . . .'

'No gossip?'

'Gossip?'

'Well . . .' The Chief Inspector was embarrassed. 'Anything odd in his private life that might have made him rather . . . reserved?'

'He wasn't a homosexual, if that's what you mean—at least, I wouldn't have said so, would you, Felicity? Felicity's better at this sort of thing than I am, but I really don't think so. Florence is very much a village, you know, everyone knows everyone else's business and anything of that sort would be known—plenty of it going on, of course . . .'

'So you think he was just a reserved person, no dark secret?'

'Well, if he had a dark secret he must have gone to very great trouble to conceal it because being reserved wouldn't do it, not in Florence. You might try the English Library, you know. English books cost a fortune here so if he was a reader he would go there—for the newspapers, too, dreadfully expensive to buy. Poor Felicity has to make do with one a week—she likes to do the crosswords, you see, but we couldn't possibly afford it, not every day. Well, look, I must be getting over to the Consulate, put up the banns for a wedding. See you about seven this evening, if you're not back before—we've got a carol service tonight at nine, but you'll be a bit tired, perhaps . . . Best of luck anyway . . . Funny chap altogether, really . . .'

THERE WASN'T room for them to walk side by side so they went one behind the other up Via Maggio to the nearby bridge, and every so often, the Chief would mutter, 'Good God,' as he leaned out to avoid a great baroque cornice or a curly iron grille and then was honked at by the streaming traffic that made him dodge back in again.

'Christmas trees!' remarked Jeffreys, surprised. The trees were stacked along the embankment by the corner of the bridge where the statue of autumn overlooked them. The tallest trees seemed to be leaning over the wall to look down at the fast-flowing greenish-brown current.

Smaller trees were lined up in little tubs, and a couple in heavy furs were examining them. The vendor, standing with a coffee in his hand in the bar across the road, watched them through the traffic, calling every now and then, I'll be right with you! Just choose what you want!'

The day wasn't too cold but damp and foggy again, and from Santa Trinita only one other bridge could be seen on either side before the yellowish fog swallowed up the river and the gray and ocher stuccoed buildings that flanked and overhung it. Most of the cars coming up the Lungarno still had their lights on and their wipers going.

'Here we are,' said Jeffreys, stopping when he saw 'English Library' engraved on a brass plate. A porter directed them to the first floor. They went along narrow, thickly-carpeted corridors with black and white photographs of the Queen and of previous Directors of the library on the walls. The whole place was dark and there was a faint smell of mold. The reading room overlooked the river and its parchment lamps added their dull yellow light to the olive-colored gloom of the morning. There were overstuffed, sagging armchairs, stern marble busts, shelves of ancient books and a stronger smell of mold. A very old man was sitting in one of the armchairs near the window, reading yesterday's *Times*. He looked up, frowning, when the Italian receptionist directed the two policemen to a desk at the far end of the room.

The librarian, to their surprise, was very young. He was sitting behind a high stack of new books and he rose to greet them, holding out a soft, thin hand. He had fine, long black hair and wore a purple velvet suit with all the buttons missing.

'Chief Inspector Lowestoft, Inspector Jeffreys. We're making inquiries about a Mr. Langley-Smythe who we think might have been a member here.'

DEATH OF AN ENGLISHMAN 61

The young man waved his thin fingers about nervously:

'Do . . . do sit down . . . yes, Langley-Smythe . . . he is a member, in fact, yes . . . he was here the other day.'

'Was a member. He's dead.'

'Dead . . . ? Oh . . .'

'He was murdered.'

'But that's ridiculous. I mean . . .'

'Yes?'

'I'm sorry, I mean, of course if you say he was murdered, it's just that I hadn't heard . . . You see in Florence—'

'Everyone knows everyone else's business. So I heard. But not this chap's. Do *you* know anything about him?'

'Well, not exactly, no, I mean, I expect—'

'Used to steal the damned paper!' The ancient man from the overstuffed armchair had stolen up behind them and was listening in. 'Seen the feller do it, walk out with *The Times* in his overcoat pocket!'

The Chief looked round at the red-faced complainant and then back at the librarian. 'Did he often come here to read the paper?'

'Came every day,' interrupted the old man again. 'Sat in that chair opposite mine. Every morning.'

The Chief turned round. 'I see. So you could say you were friends?'

'Friends?'

'If you sat opposite each other every morning I suppose you chatted? At least exchanged the odd word about the weather?'

'Never spoken to the man in my life!' The old chap was astonished, 'Used to steal the damned paper. *The Times*! You ought to keep a bit of order in this place,' he admonished the young librarian. 'Want to keep that blasted woman quiet, too!'

A woman had come in while they were talking and was quarrelling in a loud falsetto with the Italian receptionist. Her face was plaster white with powder and she wore an alice band and a long black cloak. Her hair was gray but it was impossible to guess her age.

'But I need these books for my work!' She pronounced it 'may wark.'

'Signora, six months! You have to come and renew them . . .'

'Who is she?' asked the Chief Inspector.

'Miss Iris Peece.'

'She doesn't seem to be too popular.'

'Oh, she's all right. Quite a nice old bag in many ways. She's a sort of writer . . .'

'What, novels, that sort of thing?'

'Well, that's the *thing* about Iris Peece . . . in fact . . . nobody knows. Whatever it is, she's been writing it for the last twenty-odd years, according to local legend. She spends her spare time giving absolutely gruesome little dinner-parties for anybody she thinks might be able to get her whatever-it-is published. They never can, of course. The chap they used to know in publishing has always either retired or died. The rest of the guests are the usual spongers whose private incomes aren't what they were since inflation.'

'Twenty-odd years . . .'

'At least. She even invited me once, when I first came out, but I don't know any publishers so I didn't get asked again.'

'Any chance she might have known Langley-Smythe?'

'No, I think he avoided the poor old bat.'

'What about the other members? Did he have any friends that you know of? Acquaintances even?'

'Nobody. Absolutely. Read the paper and took out science fiction books.'

'Well, if anything occurs to you, anything at all, concerning Mr. Langley-Smythe, perhaps you'd give us a ring. We're at the English vicarage just round the corner—give him the phone number, will you, Jeffreys?'

The Chief Inspector moved away, looking about him and listening in on the shrieking Miss Peece.

'I cannot be expected to interrupt may wark to come round here every other day!'

'Once a month, Signora, once a month , . .'

'Here you are.' Jeffreys copied the number on to a scrap of paper. The young man seemed ill at ease. 'Is there something wrong?'

'Mm . . . well . . . yes, in fact . . . his library books.'

'What?'

'Well, he must have had two out, he always did. I'm responsible for them . . . mm . . .' The pink fingers were working nervously. 'The thing is, we close tomorrow for Christmas . . .'

'I see. Well, the Italian police are in charge but I'll see if I can get them for you. If I don't get a chance to drop them off here I'll leave them at the vicarage.' This didn't seem to suit him. 'You never go there?'

'Absolutely not! All those ridiculous old bags with their homemade cakes . . . you'd think it was an English village, you wonder why they live here.'

'Why do you?'

'Live here? Well . . . I have a friend . . . Actually, I'm doing some writing; a monograph on an almost unknown Tuscan painter. I've been working on it for some time . . . I might develop it into something bigger . . .'

'You'll be looking for a publisher yourself, then.'

'Mmm . . . Very possibly I'll meet someone here . . .'

'You don't find it . . . depressing?' Even the new books piled on the table were beginning to bend in response to the damp. 'I mean, your customers all seem to be a bit . . . strange.'

The young man looked away, clenching and unclenching his thin fingers. 'I suppose so . . . yes. But then,' he added tolerantly, 'I'm quite strange myself . . .'

'Are you ready, Inspector Jeffreys?'

'Quite ready, sir.' They walked out briskly and went downstairs to the street.

'Depressing sort of place,' remarked the Chief Inspector.

'Yes, sir, very.' Inspector Jeffreys thought he could smell the mold on his mackintosh. 'We ought to be getting along to the Carabinieri place. We'd best get a taxi. What about a coffee in that bar opposite the Christmas trees? I could phone for one from there.'

'Good idea.'

A woman with a tiny child in a woolly red hat was looking at the largest trees. The child's jumping and shouting, coupled with the warmth of the bar with its Christmas decorations and smells of fresh coffee and pastries, soon drove away any lingering odor of mold. By the time the yellow taxi braked noisily at the corner their sense of the real world was restored to them.

WHEN THE electronic gate slid closed behind the Chief and Jeffreys, their escort of the previous day was waiting for them. 'If you would follow me,' he addressed them in Italian. He walked before them, one hand on his gleaming sword to prevent it from rattling.

And cavalry boots . . . wondered Inspector Jeffreys. The same question was in the Chief's mind.

'Speak any English?' he asked the young Lieutenant. The

young officer apologized. He spoke Italian and French. When they reached the Captain's office he saluted and left them.

'Good morning,' said the Captain, rising. Carabiniere Bacci, forgiven, was beside him, ready to translate. The Langley-Smythe file was open on the desk. The Captain was looking thoughtful. When they sat down he offered them cigarettes from a carved wooden box on his desk.

'I'd prefer my pipe,' said the Chief, 'if it doesn't bother anybody . . .'

'Please. Do make yourselves quite comfortable.' He looked down at the file while the Chief was lighting his pipe. They could hear, beneath the tall windows, cars streaming past in the damp, foggy street, sounding their horns impatiently at the frequent delays. Two cars left the building with their sirens going.

'Well,' began the Chief Inspector, 'we've been having a chat with the vicar and we've been to the English library but I'm afraid we haven't got much to tell you other than that Mr. Langley-Smythe read science fiction and doesn't, as far as we can gather—I should say didn't—have any friends. I hope you've had a more profitable morning than we have.'

'A number of things have come to light,' said the Captain carefully. 'But perhaps we should begin by looking at Professor Forli's autopsy report. The weapon used, as I think I told you, was a 6.35. The bullet pierced the left ventricle and there was very little loss of blood, death being virtually instantaneous. Professor Forli puts the time of death at approximately three A.M. and this is confirmed by a witness, a child living in the building who was disturbed by a loud bang at a quarter to three. No one else heard anything, There was quite a large amount of alcohol in the blood-stream and the stomach contained whiskey but Mr.

Langley-Smythe seems to have been a steady consumer of alcohol, according to the state of his liver; we have no reason to believe that he was intoxicated, that is, in any way incapacitated by alcohol. His health was otherwise fairly good for a man of sixty.'

'Excuse me . . .'

'Certainly?'

'You've established the time of death but I presume his meal, his evening meal, would have been completely digested by then. Does that mean we don't know where he ate or who with?'

'We do, as a matter of fact. My men questioned restaurant owners in the quarter, starting from the ones nearest his home. They made a false start, unfortunately, by trying only those restaurants which they thought a well-to-do foreigner might patronize . . .'

'And . . . ?'

'They drew a blank. No one knew him. But as there was very little food in the house, and only coffee cups in the sink, it seemed certain that he ate out. They began trying the cheaper places. Apparently, he dined every night at about eight-thirty in a small place in a side street off Via Maggio, known as the *Casalinga*, the sort of place patronized by local workmen and artisans during the day and by students in the evenings. It's possible to eat a very substantial meal there for about four thousand lire. Langley-Smythe had the same table for one in a corner every night, usually eating just one course, occasionally two. He drank quite a bit of wine.'

'Always alone?'

'Always. Including, of course, the night he was killed. Paolo, the owner's eldest son, served him. He ate two courses: roast beef with salad followed by a crème caramel. He drank most of a liter of red. He was alone at his usual table and was reading an English newspaper throughout the meal . . .'

They remembered the irate old man in the library: 'He used to steal the newspaper, walk out with it in his overcoat pocket.'

'Doesn't seem to have liked spending money,' murmured the Chief Inspector.

'A foible perhaps,' returned the Captain politely. 'It often happens . . . people who live alone . . . it need not necessarily have a bearing on the case but we need to build up a picture of his life and habits. What we do need to know, more than anything, is what contact he had with people other than his lawyer.'

'He doesn't seem to have had any.'

'But he had. A number of them. The people whose finger-prints were found in the flat. There is also the question of the money, which, you will remember, was in various currencies and which didn't pass through any bank in Florence—at least, not in his own name. Let's consider the fingerprints first.' He extracted the report from the file. 'The problem with these prints is that, according to his neighbors, Mr. Langley-Smythe was never known to have a visitor, and yet we found prints on all his furniture and his pictures—prints of seven different people, altogether. Now, he may have had one visitor without anyone noticing, but not seven, I don't think. There were other prints, too—older, unidentifiable ones.'

'What you're saying is that these are not prints of some-one who broke in . . . You've checked, anyway?'

'With Records, naturally. Only one person has been iden-tified. A local greengrocer by the name of Mazzocchio. He has a van and does occasional small removal jobs on the side. One conviction for receiving, small stuff.'

'In that case,' said the Chief Inspector, relaxing a little, 'it's quite possible that Mr. Langley-Smythe had just bought some furniture and this chap Maz—Maz . . . whatever you call him delivered it?'

'Quite possible.'

'In which case there ought to be at least some furniture which has only his own prints, am I right?'

'Quite so. His desk and the two leather chairs with it, and an armchair—and the other rooms, too, of course; the different prints were found only in the living-room.'

'So Mr. Langley-Smythe treated himself to some new furniture. We could be wasting time on this.' The Chief spoke as if to one of his Inspectors, forgetting that he wasn't in charge of the case.

'We could.' The Captain was unperturbed. 'But I don't think so . . .' Sooner or later, he would have to be told about the bust. Perhaps the simplest way was to let him see it for himself. 'We're about to revisit the house—I wonder if you would care to accompany us? As a matter of fact, there's an English lady on the top floor, a Miss White, who speaks no Italian. She would, I'm sure, respond better to you than to us, if you would care to . . . ?'

'Oh yes, certainly. We'll handle that for you.'

'Thank you. We have spoken to her already, of course, yesterday, but only very briefly . . . since we were expecting your arrival . . . I hope I wasn't being presumptuous . . . ?'

'Not at all, not at all.' The Chief was delighted. 'As I've said, we're not to be considered to be here in any official capacity but any help we can give . . .'

'You're very kind.'

Carabiniere Bacci closed his brown eyes in a thankful prayer for a second after translating this. The Captain was ringing for his Brigadier. 'I've ordered lunch in the Officers'

Club.' As the Brigadier entered he rose, and then became aware, without turning, that Carabiniere Bacci was standing to attention behind him, rigid with expectation and apprehension. 'If you gentlemen have no objection,' he added, as the Brigadier took the file and saluted, 'Carabiniere Bacci will join us, as interpreter.'

And once again Carabiniere Bacci was convinced that the young Englishman, who watched the proceedings with an ironic smile and never spoke, had winked.

CHAPTER 2

TWO SQUAD CARS TOOK them to Via Maggio after lunch; one containing the Captain and a rather mellowed Chief Inspector, his expression bland, his cheeks a little pink after a plentiful helping from a whole roast loin of pork, stuffed with sage and rosemary, and a dish of potato purée and another of green salad, followed by *Gorgonzola dolce* and a *Chianti Riserva* that was very much to his liking. The car behind carried a brigadier next to the driver, to relieve the guard on the flat, and Inspector Jeffreys next to Carabiniere Bacci in the back. It was the first chance these two had had to talk without their bosses, and Carabiniere Bacci was rather taken aback by the sudden liveliness of this hitherto silent young man. A gray drizzle was falling into the river when they crossed the bridge and drew up at the traffic lights on the other side.

'Like England, this weather, but not as cold,' offered Jeffreys.

'Yes. The rainy season. It starts early in November and goes on until the *tramontana* comes.'

'The . . . ?'

'*Tramontana*. The wind that comes across the mountains. It brings clear sunny weather but much colder, of course.'

'Yes, it would be . . .' That seemed to exhaust the weather topic but Jeffreys persisted: 'You speak very good English. Learn it at school?'

'Yes, I did study it at school but mostly I learned from my mother. She had an English nanny and then an English governess, so she speaks English as well as she speaks Italian.'

It was Jeffreys's turn to be taken aback: 'And you wanted to be a cop?'

'I beg your pardon?'

'A policeman, sorry. I mean, your family . . .'

The boy flushed a little, understanding. 'My father was a lawyer and I was also to have been one, but he died when I was still at the *Liceo*. I have a younger sister who was still a baby. Things were rather difficult . . . my mother is accustomed to a certain way of life, so . . .'

'I see. Hard for you. I'm sorry.'

'No, really. It's what I wanted. I would not have liked to be a lawyer.' His brown eyes were very earnest. Jeffreys wondered if he ever smiled. Their car was stuck in a queue, inches away from a blue and white police car that had got stuck going the opposite way. Jeffreys noticed that the two drivers gave each other no nod or wave of recognition. 'Colleagues of yours?' He pointed out to Carabiniere Bacci. The other looked blankly out of the window, straight through the blue and white car. 'No,' he stated, turning back.

'Different branch?'

'Oh no. They are nothing to do with us at all.'

'They have a Plain Clothes Division, I suppose?'

'Oh yes. But so do we.'

Inspector Jeffreys couldn't resist the image that sprang into his mind: 'Ha ha! You must keep each other well-informed! Imagine what would happen if you both turned up on a job in plain clothes—and started shooting at each other!'

Poor Carabiniere Bacci looked unhappily down at his knees without replying. It was fortunate that the car lurched suddenly to a halt at that point and a loud argument ensued between their driver and that of a car which had shot suddenly out from a side street.

'Ever been to England?' asked Jeffreys brightly, when they had started to crawl along the street again.

'No, never. I have often thought of it but . . . In the summer we close up the house in Florence and take a smaller one by the sea to get away from the heat . . . For my mother and sister, you see, it's necessary . . . I couldn't really . . . In January there is usually time to ski a little in the Apennines . . . If I could afford to take all of us to England—but I'm afraid they wouldn't go. The real problem is,' he sighed, 'that Tuscany has everything—beautiful cities and museums, mountains for winter sports, beaches . . .'

'It doesn't sound like a problem to me,' said Jeffreys, who hailed from a council estate in Stoke-on-Trent.

'But it is,' explained Carabiniere Bacci. 'Because we never go anywhere else—Machiavelli made fun of our claiming to be great travelers if we went as far as Prato.'

'Where's that?'

'About twenty minutes away from where we are now.'

'It's that bad, is it?' He was being flippant, but glancing out at the rows of shutters, the overcrowded, confined streets, he got a brief but strong suggestion of claustrophobia that might overtake anyone who stayed long enough in the city—or maybe it was really agoraphobia, the labyrinth sucked you in and you didn't even want to leave. Jeffreys tried to imagine flying to London but the idea lacked reality. 'Well, it's easy enough to get over to London, if you want to,' he said, to convince himself, 'and I'll give you my address. Be glad to show you round Scotland Yard and anywhere else you fancy.'

'Would you?' The younger man seemed moved. 'That's very kind of you.'

'Be a pleasure. This is the street, isn't it? I can see the bridge at the other end.'

'Yes. This is it. Number fifty-eight.'

'Must be your first big case, I should think?'

'My first of any kind. I'm still in Officer Training School but we are sent out to do some practical.'

'Thrown in at the deep end, eh?'

'I'm sorry?' But there was no time to explain that one.

Only the meat-roaster and the corner barman were still around to come out and stand watching their arrival; the other shops had rolled their shutters down for siesta and the wet pavements were rapidly emptying. They walked into the dark flagged passageway at number fifty-eight and the guard outside the ground-floor flat saluted them.

'Any incidents?' asked the Captain.

'No, sir.'

'None of the tenants tried to speak to you?'

'No, sir . . .'

'But?'

'Small girl, sir.' The young Brigadier blushed. 'Gave me a bit of trouble on her way in from school.'

'Yes, I can imagine . . .' The Captain frowned. 'She wasn't alone?'

'No, sir. Older child and a maid.'

'Thank you. That's all, Brigadier. Go and get something to eat. We're going inside and I'll leave the Vice-Brigadier to take over from you.'

'Thank you, sir.'

'The cold room was uninviting. 'Shall I switch on the light, sir?' suggested Carabiniere Bacci.

'Do.'

The only light was the lamp with its dusty parchment shade. The two English detectives looked about them at the carelessly placed antique furniture, the oil paintings in heavily-carved, gold-painted frames leaning against the walls, the cigarette butts scattered in the stone hearth.

'The body lay here, as marked, across the bedroom door-way—if you'd like to come through you can take a look at the safe.' The Captain led the way. Without thinking, Carabiniere Bacci stepped over the chalked outline as though the bulky figure were still lying there.

It was Inspector Jeffreys who happened to notice the slightly warped hardback book that was lying between a whiskey glass and a full ashtray on the bedside table. 'May I?' he asked the Captain, and picked it up. *Planet on Fire*. 'There should be another,' he said to the Chief, and to Carabiniere Bacci: 'The librarian wants them back, if your Chief has no objection; there's probably a second book somewhere.'

The second book was found: *Out of all Time*, beneath the turned-back eiderdown. Evidently, Langley-Smythe had lain beneath his eiderdown for warmth, but not in the bed, since he was dressed. He was waiting for something or someone but not expecting trouble or he wouldn't have had the safe open or have turned his back on the visitor. The Captain gave his permission for the books to be moved. Jeffreys planned to leave them at the porter's lodge of the library building; he didn't relish another visit to the place. The Chief Inspector was examining the open safe on the wall behind the bed, the neat stacks of notes in various currencies, chiefly Swiss francs, dollars and lire.

'All used,' he remarked. 'Any papers?'

'Personal ones, of course, but nothing of interest to us— we did find the name of his lawyer and he may come up with something useful yet but, in the circumstances, I really don't think we're going to find anything.'

'Well . . . as an attempted robbery, I agree, it makes no sense . . . and since he seems to have had no . . . social life of any kind, I suppose that leaves us with this safe. Some sort of business deal that went wrong . . .'

'Yes . . . I wonder if we couldn't save some time by sending your Inspector upstairs along with Carabiniere Bacci to have a word with Miss White. I'm afraid she's unlikely to have seen or heard anything, being on the top floor, but we ought to make sure . . . And if then Carabiniere Bacci would come down and do a little interpreting for us . . .'

'Quite, yes. Good idea . . . Jeffreys, would you mind . . . ?' He was grateful for the Captain's tact. They were going to have to have a talk and the sooner the better. Things were much more serious than the Chief had expected and no tactfully cosmetic report was going to cover this lot up. He would just rather Inspector Jeffreys were not around while he decided what should be done. As the younger men left he sat down heavily in the chair where the Marshal had once sat down heavily, and reached automatically for the pipe in his mac pocket, gazing thoughtfully out through the french windows into the courtyard.

After their recent chat, Carabiniere Bacci felt able to admit as they climbed the stairs: 'My English wasn't good enough. She's quite strange, this lady.'

'This Miss White? Well, these old dears often are.' Jeffreys was the eldest of seven children, and though always in trouble with his superiors he would go out of his way to help younger men without giving it a thought or doing anything more than wink solemnly when the younger man got the credit. 'The thing to remember is, first, that a lot of what they tell you is likely to be gossip—they'll say anything to get a bit of self-importance or to get back at a neighbor, just because they're lonely. You've got to be patient, give them some attention, be willing to have a cup of tea with them—I should say coffee in your case but it's the same thing. These stairs are a bit much—how much farther?'

'I beg your pardon?' Carabiniere Bacci was too nonplussed by the first part of this speech to catch the tail-end of it.

'How much higher?' he pointed up.

'Oh yes. The next floor.'

'Right. Then, secondly, they're frightened.'

'Frightened?'

'Criminals, crime, they live alone, they're frightened of anything coming back on them.'

'I don't think . . .' But Carabiniere Bacci's vocabulary, a genteel survival of pre-war Florence, didn't run to a description of Miss White, whose footwear alone was enough to confound him. 'This door here.'

It was open again but they rang the bell.

'Come in, come in! No charge for admission!' The invisible tenant encouraged them.

Carabiniere Bacci watched Jeffreys' face.

'Is it some sort of museum?' whispered the Inspector uncertainly as they stepped into the terracotta hallway.

'I think so, yes. She says—'

'Ah! Aha! Just the thing! More visitors to help us out— can you take photographs? It's one of those automatics so it doesn't matter if you can't—you still can, if you see what I mean. Oh, it's you again, nice to see you, and brought another friend—*plain clothes*, another first! Plain clothes detective, just like Scotland Yard, you'll have to put that in the book—detective, I mean, not Scotland Yard—never had anybody from there, not that said, anyway, but of course you never know, I suppose they keep quiet about it—not much point in going about in plain clothes and then telling everybody you're a policeman—*now*, come through here and meet Mr. MacLuskie, marvelous man, wants a photograph of himself in the house next to a portrait of Landor, but he'd like me to be in it—can't think why—so if you wouldn't mind holding the camera, here you are, press that, that's all you have to do, *press*—can't tell you in Italian, been here fifteen years and can't speak a word.' She had thrust the camera at Jeffreys. She had other plans for Carabiniere Bacci. 'We'll have you in the picture with your uniform—you don't mind him being in the picture do you? You can send me a copy.'

'Don't mind at all, ma'am. It would be a pleasure.' The visitor, a large short-sighted gentleman, a prominent member of the Paris (Texas) Poetry Appreciation League, was happy to be here and disposed to oblige everybody. He had taken the picture of the poet from its hook in the hall and was standing before the drawing-room fireplace holding it rigidly before him and gazing earnestly at the dimly perceived camera and Inspector Jeffreys. Jeffreys himself, having at first been taken by surprise, was now demonstrating 'being patient with old dears' for the benefit of his young colleague. But he found that if he got the huge Mr. MacLuskie and the tall Carabiniere in view, he could only see a scrap of Miss White's gray hair between their elbows. The alternative was Miss White flanked by houndstooth check and black serge. He tried kneeling.

'Just point and press!' advised Miss White. *'Instamatic!* One of those words that turns out to be the same in Italian, I should think, let's hope so, anyway—'

'Stand still,' pleaded Jeffreys, as the gray head bobbed in and out of the frame.

'Right! Standing still! Fire away!'

Jeffreys fired.

'Marvelous! Nice to have you in it, too,' whispered Miss White, patting Carabiniere Bacci's arm. 'You must tell your friend,' she added loudly, 'that he should learn a bit of English before it's too late—he looks quite a bit older than

you. *You have to start young,*' she admonished Inspector
Jeffreys, raising her voice helpfully. 'I bet you're thirty, thirty-
three? Eh?'

'I'm thirty-two, Miss White.' The disorientated Inspector
was trying so hard to sound English that his accent became
quite distorted.

'Too old,' declared Miss White. 'If you want to learn a
foreign language you've got to start young, the younger
the better. This young man in uniform has the right
idea—look at me, can't speak a word—had everything
translated but it's not the same thing, wish I could speak
like a native—one thing is,' she added comfortingly to
Inspector Jeffreys, '*your own langauge is a very beautiful
one.* Sign the book!'

'Det. Inspector Ian Jeffreys, New Scotland Yard, London,'
wrote Jeffreys, and Carabiniere Bacci left them.

'CAN'T OFFER you any tea,' announced Miss White. 'Can't
stand the stuff, but I can give you a glass of wine or *grappa*?'

'I'd like a glass of wine.'

They were settled in Miss White's private room which
overlooked the courtyard, a tiny bedsitter which on other
floors would probably be occupied by a servant.

'Don't give myself much room, do I?' she asked, noticing the Inspector's discreet glances. 'But people come
here to see the museum, not to see me—well, some *do*,
to be honest, people who come back year after year, send
me postcards—I make lots of friends really, trouble is,
they only come to Florence on visits, always live so far
away. But they don't forget, as you can see. Marvelous
people.'

The room was decked with over a hundred Christmas
cards from people who didn't forget.

'Mostly from America, England and Australia—but, here you are, look, one from Japan, look at that, snowman with little slanty eyes, lady who translated some of the poems into Japanese—sent me a copy, too, but I don't know which way up to hold it—here's your wine. In a tumbler, don't believe in those wretched little wine glasses. *Well*, fancy him being murdered, not surprised, of course, but fancy.'

'Not surprised? Why not?'

'Well, he was a dreadful man. Shouldn't speak ill, of course, but there it is.'

'Dreadful in what way? Have his radio on a bit too loud or something like that?'

Miss White looked at him sharply: 'If that's another joke like pretending to be an Italian, I might as well tell you I don't follow.'

'No, I'm not joking—and I wasn't—'

'Probably too old. Fashions change in humor like they do in everything else. A lot of young people these days can't see the humor in Shakespeare, well—all I can say is, I'm not surprised—I invited him up, you know, invite all my neighbors, Italians too, and they *do* come. Judge came up, marvelous man, very cultured, and the nice young woman from next door, they're away, she's American, she came, and invited me to a cocktail party once, very nice young woman—too much paint on her face, I'd say, but it's probably the fashion where she comes from and then there's Signor Cesarini, well, he's been a few times, naturally, and the Cipriani, they're always busy, two children, lots of visitors and so on, but very nice people, very polite, showed an interest and no doubt they'll be popping up here one of these days—little girl came up once to tell me about the electricity going off, they learn English at school, you see, while they had some repairs done, very considerate of them, I thought, very.'

'But Mr. Langley-Smythe?' asked the Inspector persistently, reminding himself to pick her up on one of these remarks later. 'What about him?'

'Wouldn't even open his door, just enough to poke his head out and scowl at me—and so polite on the stairs, butter wouldn't melt, playing the gracious English gentleman, but when I knocked on his door—you'd have thought I was trying to rob him! No interest at all in the English poets, not a scrap, even said so, virtually slammed the door in my face. An out-and-out philistine, and such dreadful manners.'

'I see. But you said you weren't surprised to hear he'd been murdered; what I mean is, his lack of interest in your museum, his bad manners, that wouldn't make him likely to be murdered . . .'

'But he *was*,' said Miss White incontrovertibly. 'So I'm right. You can't treat people like that. Anyway . . . I don't know if you like gossip—shouldn't speak ill of the dead so I oughtn't to tell you but I'll have to now I've said that, won't I? Well, I won't say much but I *will* say that if he'd changed his clothes as often as he changed his furniture it would have been a good thing. Now then, I've said it.'

Jeffreys took a sip of wine while cautiously juggling the components of this remark into an order that would mean something. Then he remembered the fingerprints.

'Change his furniture often, did he?'

'Once a month, I should think, on average—but that suit he's had on since he came here five years ago, I'm sure of it, stains all down the front, sort of thing that gives the English abroad a bad name.'

'Leaving aside his clothes for a minute,' pursued Jeffreys, 'it's odd that nobody else noticed this new furniture—as far as I know none of the other tenants mentioned his often bringing furniture in.'

'Well, they wouldn't notice, would they, since he always did it at three in the morning? Lot of people do, of course, they have to because of the narrow streets, against the law to block them during the day, can't be helped, delivering central heating oil, for instance, that has to be done during the night, street cleaning has to be done during the night and that's noisy but there it is. What I say is, a man who changes his furniture every month is probably a crook. Have a drop more, there's plenty.'

'Thanks. Now, wait a minute,' began Jeffreys cautiously. 'How do you know all this?'

'Seen him.'

'At three o'clock in the morning?'

'That's right. I said so—no point in my telling you things if you don't listen—there's my doorbell. Help yourself to the wine; I'll show them in and be right back.'

He heard her calling enthusiastic instructions down the housephone, heard the great doors boom closed below, then a rapid volley of excited remarks echoing in the large rooms, the swift padding of sports shoes coming back toward the bedsitter.

'Now, where were we? Sorry to rush off in the middle of a sentence but these are my opening hours, four to seven, I say opening hours but I let anybody in at any time, nice to see them, only I *say* these are my opening hours, sounds more proper, more efficient, don't you think so? Hopelessly disorganized, if the truth were known, but people welcome any time, I say, now you'll have to tell me what you last asked me, I've forgotten. It's the wine, I go quite ga-ga.'

'Oh dear . . .'

'That's all right! I enjoy it! Going to have a drop more. Go on.'

'You were telling me how you knew—'

'Ah! That's right. Look out the window. Come on! Come and look out and what do you see? Light's going but you can still see. There!'

The wintry afternoon light was already fading and the shutters were closed at most of the windows in the building, except one where a light was showing behind a muslin curtain.

'Little girls' bedroom. See the young one bouncing about? Tomboy. Look down below.' They looked down on to the top of a palm tree, plants in huge terracotta pots, and, directly under the child's bedroom, in the gloom at ground-floor level, a rectangle of weak yellow light on the stone flags. Inside Langley-Smythe's flat they could see the Captain and the Chief Inspector deep in conversation. The Chief Inspector had his head down and was rubbing his hand across his face. They couldn't hear anything but presently the Captain moved in front of the Chief Inspector and stood looking out into the courtyard.

'Notice he doesn't look up. You can see your friend now, behind. Such a good-looking boy, uniform suits him. Nobody thinks of looking up; people come to their windows and they look across or they look down, funny thing, often noticed it. But noise, now, that comes up, and the higher up you are over these courtyards the worse it is. Same with the narrow streets—I stayed in a *pensione* once when I first came out here, only came for a holiday and here I still am, *dreadful* for noise, it rebounds from wall to wall and gets louder as it gets higher—that's why anybody with any money lives on the first floor.'

'Not the ground floor?'

'No, no, no, nobody lives on the ground floor, that's for shops, garages, storage, not for living in—anyway, I'm a light sleeper so they always wake me. Got up once or twice when

I've heard them banging and clattering and I've seen them at it as plain as I see those three down there now.' Both the Chief and the Captain were at the window now and the Chief was lighting his pipe.

'And what did you see exactly?'

'Furniture removal. Pictures and statues, too, and you won't believe me when I tell you that I could *swear* one of the men who comes is my greengrocer—I bet you think I'm dotty.'

'I don't think you're dotty at all, Miss White,' said Jeffreys, who had thought so up to now but was rapidly revising his opinion.

'Most people *do* think old women are dotty, English people, anyway, and I'm seventy-two, that's why I wear these shoes, keep me going, but I'm sure that man's my greengrocer, good mind to ask him. Couldn't, of course, can't speak a word but the shopkeepers round here know what I want better than I do myself. Excuse me.' She shot away suddenly, her accustomed ear having caught the sound of visitors ready to leave. Jeffreys stood still by the window, looking down thoughtfully. Despite himself he was intrigued by this whole story, and rather taken by Miss White.

'Here we are! Back again. Have to keep popping in and out, can't help it during opening hours. Now, where were we up to this time, I suppose you know?'

'You were telling me about your greengrocer.'

'That's right, and another man, carrying stuff in and out, don't know the other one.'

'Anyone else? Anyone who looked as though he might be organizing the thing with Langley-Smythe? Or just the removal men?'

'Well . . .' For the first time Miss White hesitated.

'Yes?'

'Well, I don't know what to say. There *is* somebody else. There *was* I suppose I should say, but I never saw him properly, just once from behind . . .' She looked down at the rectangle of light, frowning.

'But you think you recognized him?'

'I did think so but I have to be honest; I never saw him except once from behind and I could be wrong so I can't say. Be a terrible slander if I was to be wrong and it was only a glimpse. No, I can't say *truly* that I recognized him so I'd better keep quiet—be a terrible slander and I'm not sure, it was just a momentary thought, no.'

She was not to be moved. They came to the night of the crime.

'Yes, usual time. Woke me up—well, I suppose it must have been the shot that woke me up this time—but I didn't get up. I mean to say, after more than four years I'm used to it, never thought.'

'Four years? And did you never think of telling the police?'

'I couldn't do that. Imagine me trying to explain that I'd seen my greengrocer going in and out in the middle of the night carrying furniture—and all in Italian—I wouldn't have known where to start. I should think they'd have locked me up, if anything. Dotty old dear, they'd have said—and don't tell me you wouldn't have said the same, you needn't blush, I've seen you giving my shoes funny looks but when you get to my age it's either be comfortable and keep going or be dignified and sit in a chair all day and I know which suits me. Anyway, there might have been a perfectly sensible reason behind it all. Kept an eye open, though, just in case. Always do keep an eye open. National pastime here, you know, watching what goes on. I don't need a television, I spend many a happy hour in the little bar on the corner with a coffee, watching the world go by, and I have a terrace at the front overlooking the piazza. No need at all for a television.'

'Obviously not. Now, what about the shot? You said you heard it?'

'Couldn't say yes, couldn't say no. I said I thought that's what woke me up but by the time I was awake, of course, whatever it was had stopped. Thought to myself: There goes my crooked greengrocer and that shocker downstairs, and went back to sleep. Pity, isn't it? I mean, the one night I *should* have got up and had a good nosey, but there it is.'

When she showed him out she remarked: 'I just wonder why those two Carabinieri didn't mention this when they were here yesterday. Can't keep a thing like that a secret in Florence. Could have told them all about it if they'd said . . . not in Italian, of course, but even so . . .'

The Chief's in for a little surprise, thought Jeffreys as he ran down the stairs, and he isn't going to like it, not one bit.

The guard saluted and opened the door for him, but Jeffreys paused on the threshold, staring. No one was speaking at the moment he entered but there was an almost palpable tension in the air, a tension that Jeffreys recognized. The three men had rearranged themselves so that the Chief had his back to the door. He was leaning back in his chair and was wreathed in blue smoke like a genie. Suddenly he heaved himself round and presented an excited, slightly flushed face: 'Jeffreys! Come in, come in and tell us all! D'you know,' he said turning back to the Italians, 'this is the most interesting case I've known for years!'

CHAPTER 3

'"UNAUTHORIZED COMMERCE IN PRECIOUS objects,"' recited the perfect student. '"Clandestine commerce in antiques!" Articles 705 and 706 of the Penal Code.'

'Now why,' asked the Chief, 'couldn't he just set himself up as an authorized antique-dealer, if that's what he wanted? Was it just a question of tax-dodging?'

'More than the usual tax-dodging,' the Captain explained. 'He could, in fact, have set up as a dealer but he would have been up against a great deal of red tape. He wouldn't have been recognized as a competent person to run such a business for one thing—any person here wanting to open even a grocer's shop has to prove his competence before he gets a licence from the local *Comune*. For anyone with no previous business experience there is a course on book-keeping, tax laws, hygiene, fair trading, etc., with an examination at the end of it. Failing that, it's possible to nominate a qualified person as director of the business. However, here we have something much more complicated. Carabiniere Bacci . . . ?'

Carabiniere Bacci translated and went on to explain the complicated laws governing the exportation of antiques: 'Many of the world's great art collections are built on art-works stolen or secretly exported from Italy. Such collectors are powerful people and, although the works are proven to have been stolen they refuse to return them except on payment of their market value which we cannot afford—although sometimes a rich businessman in the north might pay for the return of a stolen painting or sculpture to the church or museum from which it was stolen.'

'A nice gesture,' commented the Chief.

'No. He makes a *bella figura* . . . can you understand this? It is good for him and for his business, politically good . . .' He said it without rancour. 'So, because of this continual plundering of our national patrimony, a law was passed in 1939 to cover all aspects of this problem. Now it is forbidden to export antiques or works of art without a permit for each piece from the Ministry of Fine Arts. If the permit is granted an exportation tax is payable, the percentage rising with the value of the object; it may be as much as thirty per cent. In the case of works of art or craft which are important or fine enough to be considered part of the national patrimony— whether in public or private hands—the permit would be refused. Such works must, by law, be registered with the Ministry and may not be sold, moved or in any way changed or restored without permission. Registered works like this one'—he indicated the Majolica angel—'have a Ministry seal, as you can see, and are checked on at regular intervals by a competent person from a State gallery in the area.'

'What happens to this one now?' asked Jeffreys. 'Can't you return it to the owner?'

Carabiniere Bacci looked to the Captain who shook his head and explained: 'We can't move it at all without direct permission from the Minister, which should arrive soon. Even then we cannot return it to the owner's villa because the Signora is still away and the servants, who were evidently involved in the theft, have vanished, probably panicked when they heard about the murder. Since the villa is empty and unguarded, it is not a fit place to return such a valuable piece to. As soon as permission arrives it will be taken across to the Palatine gallery at Pitti.'

The same thought struck both Englishmen—permission from Rome for the police to move a terracotta bust a hundred yards!

'Once it's out of here,' continued the Captain, 'we shall no longer be directly concerned. There is a nucleus of Carabinieri in Rome dealing solely with this sort of case; they have taken over and will keep us informed—that means they will be checking on all other villa thefts in this area and watching customs for incoming pieces . . .'

'*Incoming* . . . ?' the Chief repeated on receiving a translation. 'I'm sorry, I don't follow . . .'

'I can explain . . . if I may, sir?' Carabiniere Bacci looked at the Captain, who nodded. 'It's quite a common trick. I told you that well-known collectors feel free to defy the Italian law, especially as their own countries have no laws forbidding the import of antiques, but these days most people prefer not to put their respectability at risk by buying illegally exported works. The only things that can leave the country legally are those that came into the country with a temporary import licence—pictures on loan for an exhibition, for example—these, although they may be Italian in origin, are obviously allowed out again. This can be used by a dealer wanting to export illegally—he smuggles the things out, brings them back in with a temporary permit and the buyer can then take them out. In the case of a registered dealer, naturally, we can keep a check. It's impossible to keep a constant check but sooner or later he would be caught and liable to huge fines and a prison sentence.'

'And this is where our friend the clandestine dealer comes in, is it? Langley-Smythe, in this case.' The Chief was feeling for his matches, for his pipe had gone out while he sat motionless listening to all this. He didn't take his eyes from Carabiniere Bacci.

'Yes, the clandestine dealer is, of course, not subject to any checks. He only requires space and contacts, chiefly a contact at a customs post who can let the goods out and give them a perfectly correct import licence as they come back in. But that's as far as he can go in the deal. The buyer must have an invoice with a registered dealer's name on it, have paid the normal tax, etc'

'It's complicated enough,' murmured Jeffreys, scratching his head.

'Everything you do in this country is complicated,' pointed out the Captain, when he heard this, 'legal or illegal, and there was a great deal of money involved as you've seen.'

'So,' the Chief leaned back and got his cloud going again, 'this flat is a little center of commerce. Very nice. Hence the various fingerprints on everything in here except his own desk and chair, as it were. Which brings us to Mr. X, the legal dealer, not to mention Mr. Y, the crooked customs officer, not to mention the missing couple.'

'We needn't worry about the customs end or the missing couple,' pointed out the Captain. 'As I've said, they'll be tracked down more easily by our people in Rome. They often know about such people already but lack any concrete evidence. What I want is that dealer.'

'The man Miss White saw but doesn't want to name,' put in Jeffreys. 'You could pull in the greengrocer, of course.'

'I could,' agreed the Captain, 'but he's our only link and as long as no one knows that we're on to him we're one step ahead. I've already got men out in this quarter doing spot checks on the books of all the dealers to see if anyone has been exporting an unusually large amount of stuff. That will cause a stir and possibly get us some information without suggesting that we suspect anyone in particular.'

'And do you?' asked Jeffreys.

'Yes, I do, but like Miss White I'm cautious. If I move in on him without evidence I'll never get a warrant.'

'Well, according to what you've just told us about this nice little arrangement'—the Chief waved his pipe around the room—'you can't pin anything on him if you do know who he is.'

'I'll pin a murder on him, if he's responsible for it,' said the Captain grimly.

They had almost forgotten that one inexplicable fact. The arrangement seemed to be perfect, it had worked smoothly for years, but the Englishman was dead. They were silent for a moment.

'It seems to me,' began the Chief, after prodding carefully at his pipe bowl with a spent match, 'that in your position I'd be inclined to pick up our Mr. X on a smallish charge—shouldn't be difficult—and keep him under lock and key for a while. Somebody else might decide to talk, if he doesn't. Or vice-versa, you arrest your greengrocer and put a bit of pressure on him, suggest he might be left to take the rap for the whole thing . . .'

But Carabiniere Bacci had quickly translated the first part of what the Chief had said and both Italians were shaking their heads before he had finished speaking.

'I can't do anything like that,' explained the Captain, 'because if I arrest anyone connected with the case at all, I shall have only forty days in which to complete my evidence, after which the Instructing Judge must take over. I should need a very strong case indeed before I applied for a warrant.'

'But that's practically preventing you from doing your job!'

'It's preventing me from harassing the innocent on trumped-up evidence, from running a police state, to put it bluntly.'

'It looks like preventing you from catching a villain.'

'It might. But remember that our court debate, unlike yours, is pretty much of a formality. If I get hold of that man I'll keep him.' Something in the Captain's pale solemnity shook even the Chief. To the Chief a villain was a villain; you could take liberties, so could he, but only because he had a fair chance in court. The Captain was scrupulous; he took no liberties but he looked like giving no quarter. The Chief decided he wouldn't like to be in Mr. X's shoes. Well, it wasn't his problem; his problem was over. The Chief's problem was that he liked things black and white and he liked things played by the rules, and there were too many gray areas around him these days. He knew where he stood personally, he wasn't going to stand by and see his country insulted, disrupted, untidied, by wildcat strikers, scruffy students or violent immigrants. His instinctual need for order and quiet was deeply felt. But it was a gray area in which you could never be wholly right, there were no rules, no villains, no 'fair cops'. It had been the same with Langley-Smythe; the Chief had known he was being used but that was his job, and he was bound to protect the interests of a fellow-countryman against foreigners who might use him as a scapegoat for any amount of villainy. But it was vague; it was gray. That safe full of illegally imported money, that stolen bust with an indisputable government seal around its neck were like a tonic to him. The man was a villain. The rules were in operation; if they were Italian rules and not English, at least they were rules. In return for his sudden, overwhelming cooperation the amazed Captain had agreed to keep the foreign press at bay until English interest in the case had died down. Langley-Smythe had been more than justly punished for his sins and there was no point in hounding the dead. His property would probably be confiscated and the matter closed. As for how much the family had known . . .

Jeffreys, who had only ever seen the Chief operating in the gray areas, was even more amazed than the Captain. Every now and then he glanced covertly across at the Chief's placidly cheerful face. 'It's funny,' he said to Carabiniere Bacci, 'that nobody other than Miss White ever saw Mr. X. You'd think after four successful years they'd have got a bit careless about their meetings . . . could have phoned each other, I suppose, apart from the night visits . . .'

There was something troubling the back of Jeffreys's mind; something he had meant to ask Miss White in that connection but he'd put it off until after hearing the more important part of her story and now it had completely escaped him. He was obliged to give it up. If it did turn out to be something important he could always go back up and ask her. It was, in fact, but it also turned out to be a very long night and he never did find the time.

THE FOUR men sat for some time, notebooks on their knees, in the dimly-lit room, as the dusk outside in the court-yard faded to darkness and smoke from the Chief's pipe eddied slowly about in the gloom near the high ceiling. Some things at least were established: Langley-Smythe had been expecting his visitor, had still been dressed under his dressing-gown, whiling away the night with a science-fiction book and a bottle of whiskey in the bedroom, covering himself with the eiderdown to keep warm. The night guard did a round at about three, which was, no doubt, the reason why Langley-Smythe remained in the bedroom rather than by the fire which was the only source of heat in the flat; a light in the living-room would have been visible under the door when the guard left his ticket. Once the guard had gone, and

his departure as he banged the great door to, would be easily
audible to anyone in the building, Langley-Smythe was free
to open the door and let his removal men in.

'But he must have come out to open the street door, sir,'
put in Carabiniere Bacci hesitantly. 'There's no electronic
switch in his room.'

The Captain frowned. 'The man I suspect of being our Mr.
X,' he said slowly, 'could have done it from upstairs.'

'Someone in the building,' the Chief pondered.

'Yes . . . but it makes it all the odder, you know, that
nobody ever saw them speak or visit each other.'

'But not so odd,' said Jeffreys, 'that Miss White thought
she recognized him and didn't like to say . . .' But she had
said something . . . Jeffreys could swear it was something to
do with one of the other tenants. The Captain was going on:

'Let's assume that the removal men rang, and were let in
by someone upstairs, someone who came down here and
joined them at Langley-Smythe's door. Once inside here
somebody shot him.'

'But not immediately,' pointed out the Chief. 'They didn't
just step inside and shoot him, he was shot in the back going
into his bedroom, so we need to know what went wrong and
what he was going into the bedroom for.'

'To the safe,' suggested Jeffreys.

'But what for? Not to get money out, surely? According to
what the Captain's told us, they would be paying him a cut,
not the other way about; the dealer made the sales. Any
money changing hands would be going into the safe, not
coming out, and he was empty-handed.'

'What if they had paid him,' said Jeffreys, 'and taken the
money off him after the shooting?'

Carabiniere Bacci put this to the Captain but he only shook
his head without answering. 'Why,' he murmured to himself,

'should they quarrel? And why should they leave all this stuff here when they had a truck outside ready to take it away?'

'Well, if a quarrel broke out suddenly and ended in the shooting,' pointed out the Chief, 'and I'd say it must have done because you don't set out to kill with an amateur weapon or aim at the heart, as you've said yourself, then they'd hardly hang about long enough to deal with all this stuff after the shooting.'

'But this—' the Captain laid a hand gently on the angel's head—' this is something else. They must have had a customer waiting for it or it would never have been stolen, a customer who had already paid a large deposit for the risk they were taking. There's no question of this getting any export licence, it's another class of operation altogether and it had to be done quickly, it's finished now. So why did they leave it, why . . . ?'

He got to his feet and paced about, coming to rest in front of the french windows. Staring before him, he saw the dark wall on the opposite side of the courtyard and, in the middle of it, a rectangle of yellow light at the level of the second floor. The shadow of a small figure was bouncing up and down in the patch of light, throwing something up and catching it. The Captain turned suddenly and snatched up the telephone receiver from the Englishman's desk. His free hand flicked in Carabiniere Bacci's direction. 'Go upstairs to the Cipriani on the second floor and find out if that child switched a light on when the noise woke her. You'll probably find that the answer is yes, since she was able to tell us what time it was—but check that her clock isn't luminous . . . Hello? Get me the radio room, will you? . . . Hello . . . yes, it is . . . well, we may be getting somewhere—take this message, I want it sent immediately to the men who are questioning antique-dealers in *Quartiere* 3—and give it exactly as I say it: Cancel previous order. Langley-Smythe case closed, repeat, closed, for lack of evidence. Inform all dealers, including those already visited, and return to base. Repeat it to me. Good. Send it out exactly so. When the men get back get their Chief to call me here, 284393, for further orders. I shall need them all night . . . I know and I'm sorry, but there's nothing I can do. I need them. Thank you.'

All over *Quartiere* 3, radios crackled into life, interrupting strained conversations in the quiet, elegant antique shops with polished marble floors and great copper bowls of red and white poinsettia in the Via Maggio, among the stacked-up furniture and bric-à-brac of tiny shops in Via de' Serragli and Via Santo Spirito, in the varnish-smelling restoration workshops with Christmas greetings written in glitter on their dark windows in tiny alleyways off Via delle Caldaie and Via Maffia. Officers closed up the dealers' ledgers, passed on the unexpected message, went out to their motor-bikes and switched on their headlights while the evening shoppers turned to gaze at them curiously. Dispersing among the long, narrow streets, they retraced their paths and revisited the dealers they had seen. 'You can forget it; nothing to worry about, the case is closed.' Within the hour they had reconvened and were roaring across the bridge toward Borgo Ognissanti. The fog had vanished and the rows of iron lamps shattered the black surface of the river with brittle light.

'Cesarini, eh?' said the Chief thoughtfully. 'And you really think he'd be fool enough to come down here?'

'I think he might be greedy enough and he must be tempted, if only to see what we've been doing, how much we've found out. If I told him myself that the case was closed he'd be suspicious, he's not a complete fool. But these dealers are like ants. Cesarini wasn't on the list of dealers to visit because I've already been there myself. The story will get back to him by hearsay within minutes, I should say, and he *must* be tempted when he gets back and sees the place deserted—that's if I'm right, of course. I haven't one scrap of real evidence against him—ah, Carabiniere . . .'

Carabiniere Bacci was in the doorway, his face flushed from running up and down the stairs and from excitement.

'Yes, sir. She switched on her lamp; the clock isn't luminous.'

'Right. Then it's more than possible that the light was what caused them to panic.' The Captain sat down in the leather chair in front of the desk and began beating the arm of it softly with his fist, sending up little clouds of dust as the Marshal had once done. 'And still, and still . . . I cannot believe that nobody ever saw them together . . . four years . . . it isn't possible, you can't get away with a thing like that, not in Florence; people here know what you're up to before you know yourself . . . Even in a house like this one, they may never speak to each other but they would still *know*, just as the English lady knew . . .'

The telephone rang.

'Speaking. Yes . . . good . . . exactly, I'm hoping that the dealer we're looking for might turn up here during the night. We'll go and get a bite to eat and then lock ourselves in here and send the guard away—yes, he is fortunate, you don't need to say it, I am sorry but I'm going to need your men all night because I've no hope of getting any others . . .'

Usually it didn't matter; with half the population on the move toward home, *la mamma* and Christmas dinner, criminal activity was as scarce as the policemen left to deal with it; only the traffic police expected extra work. 'When it comes down to it,' the Marshal had often said to a sceptical Carabiniere Bacci, 'we're all Italians.'

'Keep them out of sight down a side street near the piazza, a squad car and two motor-bikes should be enough—and a plain clothes man in the piazza itself to keep watch for them and be in touch with the others—no, that's not necessary; if anyone comes in we'll hear them. The man we really want is probably in the building or will be, and there are four of us here, but two others may turn up and that's where you come in—if you see them come out in a rush, block them. It's possible they may be armed so your men should be protected . . . yes . . . right, that's all.' The Captain put the receiver down and looked at his watch, 'Well, gentlemen, I think we should get something to eat and be back here before the shops close at eight. And I hope I'm not wasting everyone's time.'

'I don't think so,' said the Chief, getting up stiffly from his chair. 'And I think I'd better telephone the vicar, if you don't mind, as we won't be going there to eat.'

He rang the vicarage.

'Felicity *will* be disappointed not to see you, and we're having shepherd's pie, too. Ah well, I expect it can't be helped, this sort of thing, in your job—now you've got a key with you, in case you're late back? Only, we're usually in bed by elevenish—and do help yourselves to a cup of tea when you come in . . .'

When he put the phone down the Chief blinked to find himself still in Italy. He hadn't much hope of getting that cup of tea.

The nearest place to get a quick dinner was the *Casalinga* which the Englishman had patronized, just round the corner, for the Neapolitan in the Piazza already had a crowd of young people waiting for the pizza which he made in the evenings.

There were few people dining so early in the *Casalinga* and the proprietor's wife laid a clean white cloth for them at

a table near the window in the back room. There was no
view, just the stone wall opposite, beyond the thick lace
curtain and a red 'Greetings' sticker on the glass.

Paolo the proprietor's fat son appeared, bulging under an
immense white apron. He had brown curly hair and a stubby
pencil stuck behind his ear.

'*Stracciatella*,' he announced, bearing down upon them,
producing a notebook from under the great apron and sliding
out the pencil in a business-like fashion.

'What about a menu,' muttered the Chief apprehensively
in Jeffreys's ear. 'We want a menu; I don't like—'

'Tut, tut!' Paolo wagged an admonishing finger at him, for
he was a thoroughbred Florentine, '*Stracciatella!* Good fresh
broth, eggs laid ten minutes ago, whole thing prepared by *la
mamma*. Four. Four *stracciatelle!*' He bellowed the order without so much as turning his head.

'And what else has your mother made for us?' asked the
Captain respectfully.

'*Cotechino* and lentils,' announced Paolo promptly.
'Specially for Christmas. But will they like it? No. English,
aren't they? I'll bring them calf's liver in butter and sage and
some roast potatoes. All English people like potatoes. Green
salad? Green salad. A liter of red. Water? Liter should do you.
Fizzy or flat? Flat, the other's bad for you. I'll bring your bread.'
The pencil disappeared behind the brown curls and he was
gone from them, bellowing their order as he rolled along the
aisle between the unlaid tables with their checked oilcloth
undercovers.

When he returned with a basket of rough country bread
and a jug of wine, he slapped both on to the table and bent
to look in the Chief Inspector's face. 'Don't worry so much!'
he admonished the Chief severely. 'You'll eat well here!' He
dropped into his bit of restaurant English: 'Many English

customers! All eat well! Potatoes! Good red wine for the cold weather! All right?' He patted the astonished Chief's shoulder and poured him out a tumbler of wine and pushed the bread toward him. 'Eat!' was his final command before he rolled cheerily away again to the kitchen.

'Well,' said the red-faced Chief, 'he seems to know his job. I wasn't sure about having any more wine but I'd better do as ordered.' He broke off a piece of bread and the two Florentines watched him. For the first time, Jeffreys noticed, they were smiling.

'WE'LL TAKE these with us,' said the Captain a short time later. Fat Paolo tipped the basket of tangerines, walnuts and dried figs into a brown paper bag.

The trattoria was filling up with students, all of them loaded with large bags or folders, bringing in the cold air with them. In the front room they were noisily rearranging tables and calling out to the groups milling in the doorway, 'Over here! Gianni! There's a place!' All of them ordered *pasta* and most of them *cotechino* and lentils. It was their last meal together of the term. 'Paolo! Three *spaghetti al sugo*! Paolo! There *must* be *tortellini*, it's Thursday! And *pasta corta* for Silvia! Paolo! Come back, it's four *spaghetti*! Four!'

And the fat boy bumbled good-naturedly from table to table, tossing them bread and scribbling in his book, allowing a little grin to escape him when the girls pulled at his apron or jumped up to rumple his curls and change their orders as fast as he could write them.

One or two solitary old people sat at small tables in corners, old men of the Quarter wearing black berets and munching slowly at their *spaghetti* with toothless gums. A leathery old tramp with a long gray beard was dipping hunks of bread into his big bowl of minestrone at a table behind the door.

There was an empty place for one at the back of the room beneath a watercolor of Piazza Santo Spirito. None of the students thought of taking it, but eventually fat Paolo stuck the little table on to the end of a bigger one because the crowd of hungry students was swelling every minute. He turned the solitary chair round with an apologetic shrug at the Captain as the four policemen passed through the front room on their way out.

There were more young people outside, gossiping and riding up and down the street on their noisy mopeds to keep warm.

'It really has turned cold now,' said the Chief, turning up his collar and seeking a pair of gloves in his pocket. The slit of sky visible between the high buildings was black and speckled thickly with winking stars. An icy wind took their breath away as they came to the corner of Via Maggio. 'The tramontana,' said Carabiniere Bacci, walking beside Jeffreys. 'Tomorrow will be beautiful.'

They could see the lights still on in both of Cesarini's shops, but others were already closing, their metal shutters already half down and the last customers stooping to get out. The two vigili were starting their last round of the evening, supervising the closing of the shops, stopping for a chat at some of them, rapping on the shutters of those who were pretending to be closed. A man was struggling to tie a huge Christmas tree on to the roof of his car. The familiar noise of the rolling metal shutters caused people to quicken their pace. It was the sound of the end of the day and of supper. For the first time, the two Englishmen felt homesick. They finished the short walk in silence, and in silence turned into the dimly lit entrance of number fifty-eight. The guard was dismissed and the four of them went through to the bedroom so as not to show a light. They closed the outer and inner shutters in the hope of keeping out some of the cold but they could see their breath, and the chairs which they had brought in from the living-room were colder than their hands.

As they sat down to wait, the Captain's hand went to his Beretta.

THE MARSHAL was asleep in his darkened bedroom. The relief Brigadier had left, but before going he had driven the station Land-Rover down to the Piazza and brought back a crate of mineral water, a loaf and some black olives. The Marshal had been unable to swallow any food but, in his feverish condition, he was grateful for the supply of water. The crate standing by his bed gave him a feeling of security. The Brigadier, a Sicilian himself, had not had to be asked. The Marshal's office telephone had been connected to an answering service, transferring his calls to Borgo Ognissanti so as not to disturb his sleep.

NEVERTHELESS, HIS sleep was uneasy, his fever high. The same dream of trying to get home recurred, a dream of struggling across a burning sandy plain which swayed and rolled beneath his feet sickeningly. He knew he was trying to get home for Christmas. Sometimes trains passed by in the distance, going his way, sometimes they passed quite close by, but never close enough for him to get on them. They were all full, piled to the ceiling with luggage, overflowing with families. People were hanging out of all the windows waving empty bottles, as they do on all southbound trains, calling for someone to fill them with water. Sometimes the Marshal sensed Cipolla, the little cleaner, struggling along beside him in his black cotton overall that was too short for him in the sleeves. Why should he be with me? wondered the Marshal.

Where is he going? But the effort of asking seemed so great it hurt his burning head. I'll have to ask him, even so, he thought, I can't just ignore him. But when he finally managed to open his mouth that was so hot and dry, the wrong question came out. 'Where's your sweeping brush?' he heard himself ask stupidly. 'And your bucket?' But it didn't seem to matter to the little man; he answered, as if it had been the right question: 'To the funeral.' He didn't hear me, then, thought the Marshal. He's guessing. But whose funeral? His wife's, or the Englishman's? 'I can't come with you,' he said, 'I have to get home, it's Christmas.' They were both panting, stumbling on the hot, swaying sand. Why should it be hot like this at Christmas . . . ? A fever, it was a fever . . .

Sometimes the Marshal's glittering eyes would open briefly and take in the pale walls that were just visible in the dark, but the room swayed and rolled as nauseatingly as the sandy plain. He had to close them again and resume his wearying journey south that continued deep into the long night.

CHAPTER 4

IT WAS MIDNIGHT. THE muffled sound of the bells of San Felice filtered through the double shutters of the Englishman's bedroom. None of the four men had wanted to sit on his bed and they were all sitting stiffly now in their uncomfortable chairs, in silence. Earlier in the evening, there had been noises enough to listen to, coming from the courtyard, crockery being clattered, drains gurgling, the familiar theme of the eight o'clock TV news, laughter, a short quarrel, more crockery. They had heard the Cipriani's fat little girl squeaking and chanting and her mother's voice: 'Giovanna! Stop that! It's time you were in bed! If your father hears about this . . .' Then more TV music, echoing rifle shots ricocheting round the courtyard, thundering hooves, a cavalry horn. During the quieter parts of the cowboy film, an old, crackling record of Gigli singing Verdi, coming, no doubt, from the Judge's flat. Later came a sound of shutters banged closed, more drains gurgling, a few remarks called from room to room, then silence.

No one felt like speaking, too tired to make the effort because it meant translating, or saying things very simply, and by the time some trivial remark that might help pass the time had been mentally translated or reduced to less collo-quial terms in the would-be speaker's mind, it never seemed worth saying. So they each sank into their own thoughts in the gloom, and the bag of figs and tangerines lay untouched on the bed.

'Please God, don't let me fall asleep,' prayed young

Carabiniere Bacci on whom the strain was beginning to tell, and sometimes, 'Please God, don't let me get shot because of my mother.' He tried mentally reciting parts of the Penal Code and then some tank maintenance instructions. He had preliminary exams in both Judicial and Military soon after Christmas. But his tired mind rambled uncontrollably and always came back to a vision of himself huddled darkly on the floor with a chalk mark being made around him, and his mother . . . And the other three looked so calm and indifferent. The Captain's hand was still on the Beretta which lay on his knee but his face was as impassive as ever. 'He won't want to cut a bad figure in front of them,' the Marshal had said, 'because that would upset his superiors and himself.' Was he worrying that this whole operation might be a flop? It was impossible to tell from his face . . . and the English Chief was sitting with one foot up on his knee and his shoulders hunched . . . he might have been watching television in his own living-room. The younger one just looked tired and a bit bored. Nobody else was frightened . . . yet they all seemed pale . . . or was that just the darkness that made everyone look parchment-colored. 'Please God,' Carabiniere Bacci went on praying, looking at the door, 'don't let us have to wait much longer.' And that prayer was answered.

At ten minutes to one a loud 'clack' echoed along the passage outside. Someone had opened the main doors electronically from inside the building. Involuntarily, they all four glanced upwards. They had heard no footsteps, he must have been wearing felt slippers. Quietly, the Captain let the safety-catch off his automatic and switched off the bedside lamp. But there was a second before the light was extinguished in which he exchanged a surprised look with the Chief Inspector. The look said 'Why so early?' There was a considerable risk of other tenants still being out. Signor

Cipriani, they knew, had still not come in. But there was no time to discuss it, a faint shuffling was heard outside the flat, then a pause. The four were rigid, listening. Carabiniere Bacci had forgotten to pray. Why the risk? Surely they wouldn't dare start picking the lock out there in full view of the lift and staircase? The Englishman had always been there to let them in before. Had Cesarini come down? Not in the lift, they would have heard it . . .

The flat door opened quietly, with a key. The light went on, showing under the door of the bedroom, and then the bedroom door opened. The Captain pressed the lamp switch, his gun pointing at the doorway.

'Signor Cesarini,' he said calmly. 'We were expecting you.'

Cesarini made no move. The two figures behind him stood as if paralyzed for a matter of seconds, then they skidded round and hurled themselves toward the exit. There were shouts, infuriated shouts, and sounds of a vicious struggle echoing out in the passage. Carabiniere Bacci was suddenly on his feet, his eyes bright, pointing like a hunting dog. At a nod from the Captain he shot past Signor Cesarini and joined the chase. There was a Carabiniere motor-bike across the open doorway and the greengrocer's van was outside in the road with a squad car in front of it. But only one of the men had been stopped. The greengrocer, already known to the police and too stout to run very far, had not thought it worthwhile putting up much of a fight once he saw his van surrounded, but the younger man with him had no record and he had made a desperate run, flinging himself over the motorbike with a blow to his shin that made him scream. He was half way up Via Maggio before the two motorbikes could be started up and turned round.

The fugitive was small and thin and ran like a jack-rabbit, hidden half the time in the deep shadows close to the walls, dodging the great iron loops, the curled window bars and baroque cornices that protruded from every building and threatened to concuss him. Carabiniere Bacci was running behind him, hampered by his heavy greatcoat but closing in, even so, because the man's leg was obviously slowing him. Carabiniere Bacci was panting loudly, and above the noise of his own breath he heard a siren start up behind him, then a loud, steady roar and some confused hooting. He caught at a window grille to stop himself and turned. The steady roar was coming closer. The huge orange-and-white street cleaner was coming steady along Via Maggio, blocking the entire road, spraying jets of disinfecting water all around it. One of the motorbikes had tried to mount the pavement and its rider was now drenched and temporarily blinded. The car siren had started up again, but although the street cleaner was stopping, it couldn't turn around and would take an endless amount of time to back itself all the way down the street.

'I've got to catch him . . .' whispered Carabiniere Bacci to himself, and he turned and ran on. The fugitive had reached the bridge but he was limping badly. The traffic lights at the bridge were red and a bus was waiting there. Only yards further on, by the statue of winter, was a bus stop and the man was limping toward it, looking back over his shoulder.

'No . . . ! Don't let him . . .' shouted Carabiniere Bacci uselessly. The street seemed to be getting longer as he ran and he realized he should never have stopped to look round. 'Oh God . . . *no* . . . !' But the bus had slowed and opened its rear doors and the man was on it and away over the bridge. Again Carabiniere Bacci slowed, then he began to run again, faster than before. The car and bikes had taken another route and might not even know the man was on a bus, let alone which bus. He could still do something. Racing over the bridge, he gasped as the icy mountain wind seared his lungs. He was running toward the floodlit crenellations of the Palazzo Ferroni on the other side. The bus had gone straight on but he knew its route and how to catch up with it. He veered suddenly to the right when he reached the opposite bank, ran along under the portico, dodged across the still busy Lungarno amid a squealing and honking of cars, and vanished under a dank and ancient tunnel where his thudding steps echoed.

The bus driver was whistling. It was his last trip before the depot and he was feeling cheerful, but he was also in a hurry to get home. When Carabiniere Bacci suddenly appeared, hurtling toward the bus from a nearby alleyway with his hand raised, he put his foot down just a little.

'See that?' he inquired of his only passenger who was standing behind him. 'Cops! I suppose they think you've to stop just anywhere for them, but not me. He can get himself to a bus stop like everybody else has to.' And he continued whistling.

The passenger didn't answer. The empty body of the brightly-lit orange bus was bouncing on its springs as they sped along, the ticket machine rattling enough to shake itself off its pole.

'Cops everywhere tonight,' muttered the driver, seeing the spinning light in the distance behind him. They bounced and rattled along an empty shopping street, between big sprays of Christmas lights, and made for the Cathedral, swaying round to the right by the Baptistry. A huddled group of people was waiting for the last bus. A bearded man stepped out and waved his arm.

'Don't stop,' said the passenger quietly at his back.

'Have to stop here, even for a cop, my route—'

'Don't stop!' screamed the passenger, panicked, and the driver felt steel in his back.

'Jesus Christ . . .'

'Put your foot down or I'll fire.'

The driver, white-faced, put his foot down and the waiting group got out of his way just in time, astonished. They chased after the bus for a few yards and the bearded man whipped off his cap and waved it threateningly, shouting unheard insults until they left him far behind.

The terrified driver was gripping the wheel with hands that were sweating so much that it threatened to slip through them. His leg trembled on the accelerator as he tried to keep it down and his paralyzed brain was making hopeless attempts at remembering the instructions he had been given for emergencies like this. 'Open the doors . . . open the doors . . . open . . .' but that was to let a dangerous thief get off rather than risk hurt to the passengers. This one might not be a thief, there were no passengers, anyway. And if he were a terrorist . . . ?

'Jesus, Mary and Joseph, I don't want to be killed . . . the kids . . . and it's Christmas . . . I'm going to be late home . . . oh, don't let him . . .' His back was soaked. He fixed his eyes on the smiling picture of John 23rd stuck by his window with two plastic flowers, the nearest he could get to praying. The police car that he had seen behind him had vanished. Then he saw it ahead of them, blocking the road.

'Turn!' ordered the passenger.

'I can't! I can't turn, I'll—'

'*Turn*! ramming the steel harder into his back.

The driver turned right, bumping over the pavement. The little street was hung alternately with red and white lights saying 'Merry Christmas' and blue and green lights saying 'Happy Holiday.' Merry Christmas . . . Happy Holiday . . . Merry Christmas . . . Happy Holiday . . . Merry

Christmas . . . A flashing green tree . . . a flower . . . a star
. . . then darkness.

The driver closed his eyes.

THE MARSHAL heard the sirens and they became entangled
in his fevered dreams. He was stumbling. The sandy plain kept
rising to meet his face and then dropping away underneath
him with a sickening lurch. But he was calmer now, having
fixed in his mind that this was something to be endured, and
that he must periodically get himself to the bathroom to vomit
and then resume his hot and wearying journey. The little
cleaner was still with him which wearied him even more. He
had enough to do, trying to keep himself going without worrying about his companion's grief, the dark-ringed, patient
eyes that pleaded with him constantly, although he never
looked round at them. Sometimes they were alone, sometimes
devils with pitchforks came and prodded them maliciously,
not to make them go faster, only to torment them. They prodded the Marshal mostly in the back and he was in great pain
from it. It was getting hotter. If it got much hotter they would
die. Thank God there was the crate of water under the bed . .
. and now the sirens were going, what did that mean . . . ? He
had sorted out what it was that was happening to him once
but now he had forgotten again. Something to do with a
funeral . . . or with going home . . . but where did the sirens
come in? He had lost track . . . if only he could stop for a minute and think it out. But he couldn't stop, he realized, because
it was the ground that was moving, not himself.

'Keep everything still,' he said aloud in the dark, but
nothing stayed still and the devils were poking him gleefully
as the landscape slid about before his eyes. 'What is it?'
demanded the Marshal, giving up trying to reason for himself. 'What's happening? Why can't we stop?'

'Didn't you know?' said the little cleaner's voice, although he was no longer there. 'It's the end of the world . . .'

Suddenly the Marshal couldn't stand any more.

'No!' he shouted. 'No! It is not the end of the world. I don't believe it. I did know what was wrong with me and now I've forgotten, but it is not the end of the world and, what's more, I'm just about sick of all this, sick and tired of it, night after night—and *you*'—he pointed a furious finger at the grinning creatures around him—'can get out! *Get out of this bedroom!* All of you, and don't come back! I can't stand any more and I don't see why I should—now *get out!*' He was shouting himself hoarse but they were going. 'Right. Now, we'll see whether it's the end of the world or not. In a moment, I'm going to wake up properly and drink a glass of water. End of the world! Rubbish.'

He opened his eyes, sat up, and poured himself a tumbler of water. He drank it slowly, relishing its delicious coolness. Then he got out of bed, feeling very light and peaceful. His pajamas were clinging to him with sweat. He washed and put on a clean pair. He felt more comfortable than he could ever remember feeling in his life. 'Clean sheets,' he said to himself, and he laboriously re-made his bed. There was a blissful smile on his face as he settled in between the fresh bedlinen with a feeling of ecstatic comfort. With the smile still on his face, he sank gently into a peaceful, healthy sleep.

CARABINIERE BACCI was still running. Knowing, as he did, the route of the bus, he took another of his short cuts, undaunted by his first failure, and came out in Piazza Santissima Annunziata, gasping painfully, to await the bus's arrival. It was some moments before he realized that if the bus were on its way he would have been able to hear it. Everything in the Piazza was closed and silent, the church silhouetted against the starry sky, the only other figure the motionless one of the equestrian statue in the center. He could hear his own labored breathing and his loud heartbeat. Then he heard a siren. It was behind him and receding. He had come too far. The bus must have been stopped lower down, perhaps near the Cathedral. He started running back down Via de' Servi, the tall slice of floodlit marble jogging up and down before his weary eyes. Eventually he came upon a barrier blocking a side alley and heard some commotion going on out of sight. He wandered about among side streets until he saw the front of the bus visible at the end of a narrow passageway and the turning blue light of a breakdown truck behind it. He walked slowly toward the bus. It was wedged between the stone walls of the passage and its sides were crushed in.

'Your people have all gone,' a breakdown man informed him briefly, on finally noticing him, and then began to shout urgent instructions to some invisible colleague. The lights were all out on the bus.

The Christmas lights had all been turned off by now and the streets seemed much darker than usual. What would the Captain say when he got back to Via Maggio? Carabiniere Bacci still remembered his face after the Miss White episode. And the two Englishmen . . . he could already feel the cold-eyed gaze of the older one going over him from head to foot without comment. The younger one was more *simpatico*— but he hadn't gone running after the escapees like a kid playing cops and robbers.

It took him almost an hour to trail back to Via Maggio. When he reached number fifty-eight, someone was coming out and closing the main door. Carabiniere Bacci quickened his last few steps. Then he heard the radio buzzing on and off. The private guard.

'Is the Captain still here?' he asked the guard, with as much of his crushed dignity as he could muster.

'What Captain?'

'The Carabiniere Captain who was here with two English detectives, in the ground-floor flat!'

'Not that I know of. Brigadier there outside the door, as usual, that's all. Nobody inside.'

'Have they made an arrest?'

'Arrest?'

'Yes, an arrest! Don't you know there's been an important operation on here tonight?'

'No. I don't know anything of the sort. Quiet as the grave last time I came round and quiet as the grave now. Do you want to go in? I've got to be on my way.'

'No,' said Carabiniere Bacci, 'there's no point if—'

'I'm off then.' He slammed the door and went on his way, radio crackling, and let himself into the next building.

Carabiniere Bacci noticed then that there was a light on in the bank, a light that was always on, he remembered now, so it hadn't been his fault that he didn't notice the bank cleaners that first morning. He couldn't have known without actually seeing them. So that, at least, hadn't really been his fault. Slowly he crossed the Piazza with its metal shutters closed over the shops, and made his way back to Pitti. His weary footsteps plodded up the sloping forecourt and echoed under the stone archway. He let himself into the office and sank on to the Marshal's chair, still wearing his hat, coat and gloves.

Conscientious to the last, he pulled a piece of lined, government stamped paper toward him and began writing a report. At a quarter to four he found he couldn't go on without a rest and he flopped on to the camp bed. He remembered he was wearing his hat and gloves and took them off and flung them toward the chair. Someone had removed the blanket from the camp bed so he took off his greatcoat and covered himself with it. He fell asleep immediately and the report lay unfinished on the desk. A little later, one of his soiled white gloves slid to the floor.

'WHAT DID YOU DO with the gun?'

'What gun?' Cesarini was sneering. He had a slightly wizened look about him and, although he could not have been all that old, his hair and small mustaches were white. His clothes were from the most expensive and fashionable shops in Florence but you had to look at their discreet but visible labels to tell. There was a tinge of the fairground operator about him which hand-painted silk and supple, expensive leather did nothing to dispel. He was as calm as when they had first brought him to Headquarters just before two in the morning, and the sun was up now, coming in low at the windows of the Captain's office and warming the polished floor tiles. The Captain was exhausted, his eyes sore and his face dark with beard, but he would not give in, especially in front of the two Englishmen who were sitting slightly apart from the action, hunched in their chairs. Jeffreys, too, was pale and bleary-eyed.

The Captain repeated tonelessly: 'What did you do with the gun?' The man's flat had been searched as soon as it was light, his shops were being searched now.

'You haven't told me yet what gun.'

'Yours. I suppose you keep one?'

'Yes.'

'Where is it?'

'In the shop, the bigger one. Your men will find it if they know their job.'

'They do.'

'Well, then.'

'I take it you have a licence?'

'That's right.'

'What time did you visit the Englishman on Tuesday night?'

'I didn't.'

'All right, then, in the early hours of Wednesday morning.'

'I didn't.'

'What were you going to do there, last night?'

'I've told you. I was checking my property. I have every right to look over my own property. You'd taken your guard off and I'd heard the case was closed, so why shouldn't I? I rented him a flat and that doesn't make me a murderer.'

They all blamed themselves for not thinking of it, and nobody more than Inspector Jeffreys who had meant to pick Miss White up on that remark, 'Signor Cesarini, well, he's been a few times, naturally . . .' Naturally. It had struck him at once as odd, that 'naturally.' Why should he be interested in her little museum? But he had been anxious to get to Langley-Smythe, to stop Miss White from rambling so much in her story—should have taken a bit of his own medicine and been patient. Cesarini visited all the flats because he was the landlord—all except the Cipriani flat which had been in their family for generations. Cesarini had been buying them up over the years with their tenants in them. Of course, when the tenants were asked about Langley-Smythe's visitors, nobody bothered to mention Cesarini. He wasn't a visitor. The Captain had even telephoned Signor Cipriani as soon as the hour was reasonable and asked him if he had ever, by any chance, seen Cesarini go into Langley-Smythe's flat, or vice-versa.

'Yes, quite often, I suppose, but naturally, as he's—'

'Yes. Thank you, we know that now . . .'

Naturally.

The Captain was now as irritated as he was exhausted.

'What was your business relationship?'

'What makes you think we had one?'

'You deal in a lot of imported furniture.'

'So? Your men have seen my books, if I remember rightly.'

'And found nothing illegal. The Finance Police are looking at them now.'

'And will find the same, nothing illegal.'

'But a lot that is interesting. And the fingerprints of your two friends of last night are all over the furniture in the Englishman's room.'

'That's hardly my responsibility.'

'Why were they with you last night, if you were only checking over your property?'

Cesarini shrugged.

'You refuse to answer?'

'Why should I? Am I under arrest?'

'Not yet.'

There was that, at least. The Captain had waited for Cesarini last night with every intention of making an arrest *in flagrante*, and only the key had, fortunately, made him hesitate.

Cesarini shrugged again. 'They're friends of mine.'

'Really? Their fingerprints could mean that they'll be charged with murder.'

Another shrug.

'You don't seem to be too concerned for your "friends."'

Cesarini glanced out of the window as if he were bored.

The Chief Inspector had lit his pipe and was chewing on it, concentrating, sometimes looking to Jeffreys in the hope of a bit of translation, but mostly just concentrating. This battle was the same in any language, the rise and fall of tension, the gradual building up of a peculiar intimacy between questioner and questioned that, more often than not, ended in a confession if a guilty man were anything other than a professional killer.

The Chief sensed that things weren't developing as they should.

'Mind if I have a smoke myself, seeing as this is just a social visit?' Cesarini asked cockily. Drifts of blue pipe smoke from the Chief Inspector's corner were revolving in the sunbeam that was now striking the edge of the Captain's desk.

'By all means. If you have any cigarettes.'

'Well, well, I thought you were supposed to be the most civilized cops in Italy,' said the dealer, with his eye on the carved cigarette box on the desk.

'We are,' said the Captain quietly, but not moving. 'Otherwise you might be a great deal less comfortable and cocksure than you are just now.'

'Are you threatening me?' The dealer's face reddened. It was the first reaction they had had out of him.

'Not at all; merely pointing out a fact. How much did you pay him? A percentage of each deal?'

'What deal?' Cesarini scrabbled in his pocket for cigarettes and a lighter. Just as he was about to thrust a cigarette into his mouth, the Captain said:

'How much rent did he pay you?'

The dealer stopped; he took out the cigarette slowly, looking down at the floor, then put it back in and snapped the lighter.

'Who?' he asked eventually, inhaling deeply.

'You know who.'

'I have a lot of tenants.'

'The Englishman.'

'Not much.'

'How much?'

'I don't know how much, not off-hand. Why should I?'

'Every reason. Nobody lets a flat and doesn't know what the rent is.'

'Perhaps I'm inefficient.'

'Perhaps. The people who checked your books didn't seem to think so. They thought you remarkably efficient; books beautifully kept, copies of import and export licences, invoices for every sale. Remarkably efficient.'

'Thanks.'

'How much was the rent?'

'If you know, why bother asking?'

'What makes you think I know?'

'If you didn't, you wouldn't think the matter worth enquiring about. Do you think I'm a fool?'

Yes, thought the Captain, you are. Because I didn't know. I was guessing.

Aloud he said: 'He didn't pay any rent, did he?'

Cesarini leaned back again and blew smoke at the ceiling without answering, but his face was dark, his nonchalant pose unconvincing.

'Is that how it started? You offered him a free flat?'

'Why else would anyone live on the ground floor, and in a hole like that?' he said it disgustedly.

'You don't seem to have liked him.'

'Why should I?'

'It's a little unusual to offer someone a free flat if you dislike them, even on the ground floor. What had you against him anyway?'

'He was a miser. I didn't say I disliked him but I suppose I despised him.'

'But you gave him the flat, although you despised him and thought him a miser.'

'So? That's a personal opinion. I don't let personal opinions get in the way of . . .'

'Of business, Signor Cesarini?'

'I want my lawyer here—you're deliberately twisting everything I say, trying to trip me up. I want to telephone my lawyer!'

'Would your lawyer happen to be Awocato Romanelli?'

'How do you know that?' He was wary now, though still affecting a sneering confidence.

'I just thought it might be. He happens to have been the Englishman's lawyer, too. An interesting man. I hope to have further talks with him. However, you're not really in need of a lawyer now. After all, you're not under arrest, if you remember.'

'Then you can't keep me here.'

'I can get a warrant for your arrest any time I want it; meanwhile, my men will go on looking for that gun.'

Cesarini's face visibly relaxed.

'That doesn't worry you.'

'I've already told you I've got a gun, and a licence for it, and that it's in the shop. Your men will find it and much good may it do them. You'll find it hasn't been fired for years.'

'Then why keep it?'

'Why not? I sell some valuable stuff. A shop like mine could be robbed, and robbers have a habit, in this city, of turning up in the daytime with guns, since they can't get into the buildings at night, as I'm sure you've noticed.'

'Somebody seems to have got into one on Via Maggio, unless he was in there already. And perhaps the Englishman had a gun, a 6.35 possibly.'

'Possibly.'

'What about your two friends?'

'What about them?'

'Did they carry arms?'

'You've picked them up, haven't you? Ask them.'

'I will. They weren't armed when we brought them in but just now I'm asking you. Do they carry arms?'

'No.'

'Never?'

'Not that I know of.'

'Let's return to the furniture. Your friends were frequently seen moving furniture in and out of the Englishman's flat by one of your tenants.'

No answer.

'It seems a little eccentric on his part, to have wanted to change his furniture and his paintings and statuary every month.'

'The English are eccentric, so they say.'

'So they do. We have two Englishmen with us now, but I have a feeling that they think it was eccentric of him, too, so perhaps not all English people are eccentric.'

The dealer didn't look round but he evidently seemed to feel the Chief's eyes boring into him.

The telephone rang: 'Marshal Guarnaccia at Pitti for you, sir.'

'Put him through. Good morning, Marshal. How are you? Are you sure? I see. Well, if you think you ought to go . . . you have my man there? Yes, certainly. I'm not sure, but keep in touch, will you? Ah yes, indeed—I'd forgotten him, to tell you the truth. You'd better leave him to get some rest as we're not really in need of an interpreter, at this stage, and you have my Brigadier there—oh, on second thoughts, if he's had some rest, you might wake him up and send him over to Via Maggio. We're desperately short-staffed and the man I left over there last night still hasn't been relieved. The lad shouldn't come to any harm standing outside the flat, I'll send someone else as soon as I can . . . He certainly does . . . Good thing when he gets back into school, though I must say his English has been a help. Tell him to try and keep out of trouble for about the next two hours. And take it easy yourself . . . I'd like a talk with you later if you're feeling fit . . . Yes . . . Till later, then . . .'

There was a moment's silence after the Captain had replaced the receiver. He was looking down at his own hands on the desk. They were still brown from the long summer, he thought. The irrelevance of that thought struck him; he was too tired to be questioning this man. They were getting nowhere, and yet it would be unwise to let him go away knowing that. The only hope was to worry him at least a little so that he would have something nagging at him while he waited around for a few hours. But what? The man was very confident that nothing could be proved against him as far as his dealing was concerned, and he was probably right. Everything had gone so well for years . . . But then why . . .

'What did you quarrel about?'

'Quarrel? Who am I supposed to have quarrelled with?'

'Who had the customs contact, you or he?'

'What contact?'

'Had you found someone else to do the Englishman's part? Whatever was wrong, he wasn't expecting it.'

'Nothing was wrong.'

'You admit, then, that you were dealing with him?'

'I admit nothing. And nothing can go wrong with nothing.'

'He let you in and turned his back.'

'I wasn't in his flat that night and you'll never prove I was.'

'It may, in the end, be up to you to prove you weren't. You were his only contact.'

'So a thief broke in.'

'Nobody broke in. You said yourself, nobody could break into a building like that. And nobody lets a stranger in at that hour.'

'It's not my problem. I wasn't there.'

'I am telling you, Signor Cesarini, that it may very well turn out to be your problem. There was at least one piece of stolen property in that flat.'

'Not my business, it was his flat.'

'But it wasn't. You said so yourself. He paid no rent, had no rent book, no contract. The flat is yours and he was there as your associate, not as a tenant.'

Cesarini's eyes slid to the window, as though seeking a means of escape. The telephone rang again.

'S.P. for you, sir.'

'Put him through.' The Captain reached forward and pushed the bell on his desk. 'Good morning, Signor Procuratore . . . speaking . . . Yes, indeed—could you hold the line for one moment, I have someone with me who is leaving now.' A Brigadier entered, summoned by the bell. 'Show this gentleman to a waiting-room, would you, Brigadier, and get him some breakfast.'

'You can't keep me here!'

'Enjoy your breakfast, Signor Cesarini.' He waited for the door to close. 'Signor Procuratore, please excuse . . . Well, naturally, but I haven't had time since you issued the search warrant to—The press . . . I see. No, to be honest I didn't even see what they printed yesterday or this morning either, for that—Yes, I realize that, it's just that I'm trying to avoid any unnecessary scandal about the Englishman . . . Well, yes, there is . . . No, nothing of that sort, it's all in my report. I'm

afraid it hasn't, we're still looking for it—if you could perhaps encourage them to concentrate on the episode with the
bus which is more newsworthy from their point of view,
anyway. I see . . . Well, he would be concerned, of course, but
. . . if you think that would help—No not at all, of course you
wouldn't interfere, I wasn't suggesting . . . Yes, Signor
Procuratore, I'll see to it immediately. Not at all, your advice
is always welcome . . . At three o'clock, then . . .'

After putting down the phone, the Captain closed his
eyes for a moment and gave an almost inaudible sigh. Then
he looked at the two Englishmen. Jeffreys was so exhausted,
especially from the strain of trying to follow the interrogation, that he was having difficulty remembering where he
was. He was continually smothering yawns and rubbing a
hand over his scratchy eyes and through his disheveled curls.
The Chief Inspector was chewing his pipe and staring at the
Captain, showing no signs of tiredness. He looked as though
he could go on indefinitely without sleeping if he had to, or
if he thought he would.

'No good,' he said, removing the pipe and raising an inter-
rogative eyebrow.

'No good,' agreed the Captain, understanding. He smiled
ruefully.

'Wake yourself up, Jeffreys,' said the Chief with a nudge.
'I want to talk to the Captain.' But they hardly needed
Jeffreys's stumbling efforts to understand each other. The
interrogation had gone badly and they both knew it and,
what was worse, they both knew why. The man was obviously guilty as far as the antiques affair was concerned but he
had no fears as far as the murder was concerned.

'D'you know what struck me?' said the Chief, musing, 'It
struck me that not only was he not scared, he was plain irritated. Irritated that you caught him in the flat, irritated that

business is disrupted, even irritated that the Englishman got himself killed. And yet, if he didn't do it—you don't suspect his two friends?'

The Captain shook his head. 'Not in the least. We know Mazzocchio well enough, and the other's his nephew, an apprentice plumber—I think threatening a bus driver with a bit of piping to get a free ride is about his limit, and he'll not do that again in a hurry when we've finished with him. Neither of them qualify as hired killers, not with their finger-prints all over the flat and a 6.35.'

'And that leaves nobody.'

'Exactly. Signor Nobody. Now, if you'll excuse me, I have to make a phone call. The S.P. has suggested that we drag the river at the Santa Trinita bridge on the grounds that it's the nearest point at which the escaping murderer could have got rid of the weapon.' He said it evenly but the irony came through just the same. Jeffreys caught it and was baffled.

'Does he really think you'll find it?'

'I very much doubt it but the Mayor's upset so we'd better be seen to be doing something.'

'The Mayor?' Jeffreys wasn't sure he had understood.

'Yes, the Mayor. He gives a reception every year for all the foreigners in the city. It's tonight. Most of them are English. The Mayor is embarrassed.'

'But the English . . .' Jeffreys tried to marshal some Italian words into order. 'They didn't . . . he had no friends, wasn't liked . . .'

'It doesn't matter. The Mayor is embarrassed and we are going to drag the river. But you must need some sleep. There's really no need for you to come, no point . . .' The Captain was glad enough to go, in some ways. He hardly knew what else to do.

Jeffreys' face had brightened at the thought of bed but

when he suggested it to the Chief he made no impression at all.

'No, no, no! Wouldn't miss it for the world, would we, Jeffreys? Like to see how you go about things, and so on. Besides, you never know, you might find the wretched thing! No, we can sleep any time, we'll come along with you.' And he pocketed his pipe enthusiastically.

All right, thought Jeffreys, in despair. He's a good cop. And I wish I were in bed.

'We'll come with you, thanks,' he told the Captain with a weak smile.

When the Captain had made his calls and they were ready to leave, the telephone rang once more. After staring at the receiver in a puzzled way and then frowning as he listened and trying in vain to interrupt the speaker once or twice, he suddenly offered the instrument to the Chief Inspector:

'I wonder if this is for you?'

It was.

'Felicity was worried about you so I said I'd phone—took me a long time to find you, I must say, but I suppose it's a biggish building. Of course, we thought you were in bed so it was a long time before we noticed, thinking we shouldn't disturb you. Not having heard you come in, you see, we thought you'd had a heavy night and were lying in. Eventually thought of taking you in a nice cup of tea and you weren't there so Felicity was worried . . . no . . . *no*, not a thing! Of course, I'm a good sleeper, well, we both are. We're usually in bed by eleven with a good thriller and I think I can safely say we're generally asleep by twelve. Didn't hear a sound, no. So now, what about your lunch? I see . . . *are* you? How fascinating! Well, I'll be going across to the Consulate to see about Mr. Langley-Smythe's body going back—they've had a call from the Medico-Legal Institute . . . I suppose you could take it back with you . . . Anyway, I'll certainly stop at the bridge to see what you boys are up to. What a shame you had to miss the carol service last night—anyway, we'll hope to see you at lunch. Felicity's making a bread-and-butter pudding . . .'

THE MARSHAL stood looking down at Carabiniere Bacci, his great round eyes blandly expressionless.

The Brigadier at the desk grinned: 'Have I to wake him?'

'Yes . . .' said the Marshal slowly, buttoning his greatcoat, 'wake him and send him across to Via Maggio to relieve the man on guard there. And tell him to get some breakfast on the way. I'll be back in about an hour . . .' He stood a little while longer, staring down at the crumpled, sleeping figure and then stepped outside and walked slowly under the high archway. He was shaky but he was better. As long as he didn't overdo it . . . and he wasn't going very far. When he emerged on to the car-filled forecourt, the brilliant sunlight dazzled him. He sighed and plunged a hand into his great-coat pocket, seeking his sunglasses.

'GLORY . . . !' WHISPERED the Chief Inspector. He had closed his eyes during the car ride, not sleeping, just resting them, and had been aware of intermittent flashes of brilliant light, but when the car emerged from the cold blue shadow of Via Maggio and stopped on the Santa Trinita bridge, the light prised his eyes open.

'You wouldn't think it was the same place,' agreed Jeffreys, getting out stiffly and blinking.

They felt as if, until now, they had been groping about on a barely lit, complicated stage set, on to which someone had suddenly turned all the spotlights. They stretched their tired limbs and stared. The white marble statues at each corner of

the bridge sparkled as if in movement, their heads outlined
sharply in black against a deep blue sky. Across the river
were the crenellated tops of palaces, gothic towers, ocher
façades splashed with light, dark blue shadows, orange roofs,
and a swirl of anarchic traffic conducted by a white-helmeted
vigile. All the movement was faster, all the noise louder without the muting effect of the fog, but the river was running
slowly, smooth and olive green, away toward a distant net-
work of bare trees that indicated the park. Beyond the trees,
a line of glittering mountain tops was strung across the hori-
zon like a mirage.

Having readjusted themselves to this new world, the two
Englishmen began trying to push their way through the
crowd of people hanging over the parapet near the busy
Christmas-tree seller, and see what was going on.

The divers were just going in from a black rubber dinghy
below the embankment. Elaborate rumors as to what they
were looking for were rife among the ever-increasing crowd
of spectators, some of whom carried briefcases or sheaves of
office papers, others big carrier bags from the shops across
the river, others pushing handcarts or delivery bikes. Some
drivers stopped their cars in the middle of the bridge to come
and have a look.

'Doesn't anybody round here go to work?' muttered the
Chief Inspector irritably, as he was elbowed about.

'National pastime, this,' explained Jeffreys, remembering
Miss White, and wondering briefly why she wasn't here now.

'ETERNAL REST give unto her, O Lord, and let perpetual
light shine upon her . . .'

The altar boy trailed round the coffin after the old priest,
carrying the holy water. There was a heavy 'clonk' each time
the priest dipped the aspergillum into it. The altar boy's nose

was red. San Felice church was icy, winter and summer alike; the stones of its twelfth-century walls exuded the stored cold of eight hundred winters. The slits of leaded window along one side had never been touched by the sun.

'May she rest in peace . . .'

The priest returned to the altar and the requiem mass continued.

The Marshal was sitting right at the back, although the church was almost empty. He had made his presence known, shaking hands with Cipolla, almost unrecognizable in a cheap green loden with a black armband, and then retreated to the back in case he needed to go out. He was still feeling very weak, and the deathly cold in the dark church penetrated even his heavy greatcoat. He wasn't alone at the back; a small woman in a long, old-fashioned fur coat and a woollen beret had come in, seemed remarkably pleased to see him, as though he were an old friend, and had sat down beside him. When they knelt down for the consecration, he noticed that she was wearing running shoes. He was sure then that he had seen her about often but he couldn't think where. Kneeling made him feel wretchedly dizzy and he found himself obliged to sit down and close his eyes. The heavy smell of beeswax mingled with the chilly perfume of the flowers piled in the open doorway behind him. He kept his eyes closed, breathing deeply and steadily, his large hands resting on his knees.

'Lord, I am not worthy that Thou shouldst enter under my roof. Say but the word and my soul shall be healed.

'Lord, I am not worthy . . .'

The Marshal opened his eyes. Cipolla remained kneeling; his sister and brother-in-law went up to take Communion, followed by a small group of women dressed in black who seemed to the Marshal to be at every funeral in every church in Italy . . . like vultures. An obscene thought that he tried to dismiss . . .

The tall candles on brass stands before and behind the coffin in the center aisle flickered and spat in the cold draft from the door. He could see his breath.

'Lord, I am not worthy . . .'

The Marshal found it difficult to take his eyes from the two tall flames; they began to blur into one.

'Say but the word and my soul shall be healed . . .'

Somebody ought to have closed the church door. The Marshal's head was ringing with cold, the flames were growing bigger and approaching him, overpowering him with the cloying scent of flowers . . .

'Say but the word and my soul . . .' Vultures hovering in the candlelight . . . no . . .

'Say but the word . . .'

'Here,' commanded a loud English whisper. 'Smell this. Lean on me.'

Miss White propped up the swaying bulk of the seated Marshal and thrust her smelling salts under his nose. They worked. He blinked and righted himself.

'What the devil . . . ?' He had quite forgotten where he was.

'No use talking to me. Can't speak a word. But you ought to get out into the fresh air. Bit of sunshine. I'll carry your hat.'

The Marshal allowed himself to be towed away toward the flower-filled doorway and the light of the Piazza. His eyes immediately began to stream.

'Overcome with grief,' said Miss White to the black-overalled men who stamped on their cigarettes behind the hearse when they saw people coming out. 'Going to buy him a coffee. Come on! Lean on me, if you like!'

'Signora!' the barman on the corner greeted her as she pulled her great burden in. And the Marshal—are you better? You look pale.'

'He needs a drink,' instructed Miss White. 'And so do I. Freezing in that church—*two coffees* and plenty of *grappa* in them!'

'Immediately,' responded the barman. 'Shall I bring it to the table?' There were two tiny round tables in the bar.

'*Sì!* Yes, you'd better. He needs to sit down.'

When the barman brought their laced coffee, the Marshal had wiped his eyes and recovered sufficiently to remember where he had seen Miss White before—right there in the bar, looking out at the Piazza. He had seen her from his own habitual viewing point at the corner of the church.

He looked up at the barman. 'I didn't know you understood English?'

'Me? I don't.'

'Well, how do you manage to talk to her?'

The barman was nonplussed. 'Well . . . she's been coming in here for years . . . I've never really thought about it. *Simpatica*, don't you think so?'

'She is. We met at the funeral, I didn't feel too good.'

'Ah, that poor woman . . . and no children either . . .'

'I'd like to know why the English Signora was there, if you think you could—'

'Oh, I can tell you that. Signora Cipolla, God rest her soul, used to work over there—' he nodded across at the entrance of number fifty-eight. 'Not for the Signora, you understand—although I think she used to visit her—for the Englishman downstairs—only for a few weeks—but then, Cipolla worked there himself, so . . .'

'I see.'

A chorus of furious hooting started up outside and the

Marshal, Miss White and the barman automatically went to
the open door to look out. The Marshal put his dark glasses
on.

A van was parked in the center of the triangle where all
the roads met, and a diminutive man wearing a checked
wool windjammer over paint-spattered trousers and a rolled-
up brown paper bag on his head had unloaded two hundred
large, mock-antique, carved wood, gold-painted picture
frames into the road. The young *vigile* had adjusted his helmet and gloves and was walking toward the scene
purposefully.

'Poor chap,' murmured the Marshal.

'Mmm, and he's already been in one row today,' added the
barman, lighting a cigarette. 'Coach driver, a German, gave
him hell. He tried to direct him round into Via Maggio,
scraped the side of the coach on the milk truck that had just
stopped here without him noticing—poor lad, he couldn't see
it, not from behind the coach, driver should have seen it himself, but Germans . . .' He knocked on the wooden doorpost to
indicate the intractability of the race.

'Never mind Germans,' said the Marshal, thrusting his
hands deep into his pockets. 'He's going to have to tackle an
Italian now . . .'

But the young *vigile* was intrepid. He approached the
paper-hatted man who was reaching inside the van for some
more frames, adjusted his helmet again, and said politely:
'But you can't unload these here, you know.'

The other stiffened slightly for a second and then
answered without turning his head so that he could affect
not to know who it was: 'Oh no? Well, I already have done,
haven't I?'

The *vigile* hesitated, avoiding the eyes of the nearest spectators, coughing a little behind his glove. He couldn't very

well announce pompously, 'I'm a *vigile*,' without losing face immediately, and he knew that the other would keep his back turned indefinitely, if necessary. He approached the thing obliquely.

'There's a *law* against unloading here.'

'Oh yes?' He still kept his back turned and was winking at those members of the audience who could see his face. 'And who are you that you know so much about the law?'

The crowd laughed. Round one to the driver. Capitalizing on this, the little man turned his head and then clutched at his paper hat in horror: 'My God! The *vigile!*' And he began making grossly exaggerated apologies. The crowd loved it. More people were collecting, customers coming out of the bank stayed to watch. Windows were opening high up in all the buildings. The young *vigile*'s face was red but he had been in the job long enough to know that if he lost his temper he was finished. Quietly he said, 'Move this stuff, you're blocking the road.'

But it was impossible, as the driver pointed out, to hear a word above the racket of engines and horns.

'Move this stuff! It's against the law to unload here!'

'Ah,' said the driver, nodding, and pitching his voice so as to reach the upper gallery, 'it's against the law, is it? And who made this law exactly, can you tell me that?'

'Never mind that, you just obey it!' The worst thing he could have said. The driver was delighted.

'Oh yes? What are we, then? Germans?' He turned to the crowd and swept his hands open: 'Are we, or are we not, all Italians? And are these laws, or are they not, made for our benefit? And have we, or have we not, a right to know—'

'All right, all right! The Government makes the laws and the *Comune*—'

'The Government, eh? The *Christian* Democrats,' he

explained to the audience. 'That lot down in Rome—and do these *Christian* Democrats know, do they re-a-lize, that Gino Bertellini—that's me, a Florentine, like all these good people here'—he waved a hand around to include the Marshal, Miss White, the Neapolitan and a group of American students going by eating pizza—'Gino Bertellini has to deliver these frames to that shop over there near the bank before eleven o'clock or he will probably lose his job? And have these Christian Democrats, in their great wisdom, provided him with a place to park and unload them? Well?'

'He's right,' the crowd began to murmur.

'Of course he's right,' put in the meat-roaster loudly. He was expecting a delivery of chickens to be unloaded on that very spot any minute.

'But it's the same for everybody,' began the *vigile*. 'We've all got to be equally—'

'Hello! He's a Communist!' quipped the driver, and got another laugh.

Drivers who by now had had enough entertainment were starting to rev their engines and lean permanently on their horns. Some of them put their heads out of their windows to abuse the *vigile* for not knowing his job. The tiny Piazza was clouded with exhaust fumes. An elegant driver with an enormous fur collar on his coat appeared on foot, having walked from the tail-end of the queue which stretched back to the river to enquire if they were holding a tea-party, in which case they might like to invite him . . .

'I'm doing my best!' cried the distracted *vigile*. 'And nobody takes any notice—everybody blames me, no matter what I do—if I try and shift this chap I'm a German, and if I don't unblock the road I don't know my job!'

'He's right, poor lad,' said a woman carrying a quarter of a cabbage in a plastic bag. She had a son in uniform, doing his national service.

'And what am I trying to do, *excuse me*? What do think I'm trying to do?' The driver slapped the stack of gold frames. 'Am I a millionaire who's doing this for fun?'

The crowd divided into two camps and began a separate argument.

'Marshal! Marshal!' cried the woman with the cabbage, spotting his dark bulk in the bar doorway. But the Marshal backed up, opening his hands to indicate that he couldn't interfere.

Then the gray-suited stationer stepped majestically into the road: 'Do you realize,' he boomed, in a voice that would have silenced the most tumultuous courtroom, 'that there is a funeral going on in this Piazza?'

The crowd stopped arguing.

The driver pushed his paper hat to the back of his head and scratched himself, baffled. 'What's a funeral got to do with anything?'

'It's got to do with our having some respect for the dead, for a woman, a neighbor, whose funeral is being held right now and who can't be carried to the cemetery because of the disgraceful row going on here. Poor Italy! And poor Italians who can't even have a dignified funeral because of this sort of self-centered buffoonery!'

The stationer stepped back and crossed himself slowly.

Everyone looked across at the church. It was true. The coffin had been loaded into the hearse, the wreaths with their broad purple ribbons attached on the outside. The cortège had been unable to move and the family was huddled, frozen, in the church doorway. The priest, still wearing his purple cope, had his hand on the little cleaner's thinly-clad shoulder.

'Well,' muttered the paper-hatted driver, 'I didn't know, did I?'

'You didn't care to know,' pointed out the stationer, 'whose way you were blocking.'

'How are we going to manage?' murmured the driver, beginning to shuffle the frames about unhappily. The *vigile's* mate was approaching, having walked from the bridge where he was on duty to see what the hold-up was. After a rapid conference, a compromise was reached and the two *vigili* and the driver began hurrying between the van and the shop, carrying the frames. The younger of the black-overalled men from the hearse came over to help them, and Miss White shot out of the bar in her speedy footwear and tried to pick up a frame.

'Thank you, Signora, thank you,' said the driver as he hurried past her.

'No use speaking to me,' panted Miss White, hauling the frame a few feet with difficulty. 'We're all here to help each other.'

Then a shot rang out.

The noise echoed all round the Piazza so that it was impossible to be sure where it came from. People began screaming and running for shelter in doorways, others stood staring about them, not sure what to believe. In the noise and confusion that followed, the Marshal, whose view of the church was blocked by the van, thought at once of the little cleaner—'It's the end of the world'—and began running across toward the hearse. But Cipolla was still standing there, dazed, with the priest's hand on his shoulder, and people were crying out, 'Marshal! Over here!' He swerved and made for the bank, but the bank guard came running out, gun in hand, through the glass door and turned and ran in at the entrance of number fifty-eight. 'No . . . !' whispered the Marshal, running after him. 'It's not possible . . .'

'Ambulance!' yelled the bank guard, running out again and colliding with the Marshal.

'What's happened?' shouted the astounded Marshal, coming round the corner to the Englishman's door. '*What?*'

A white-faced Carabiniere Bacci was kneeling beside a half-conscious woman in front of the lift door.

'She's been shot,' he whispered, looking up, his mouth so dry he could hardly articulate it. A plastic bag with two large bottles of mineral water in it had smashed on the floor and water was running everywhere on the flags, some of it streaked with red.

'She's been shot,' he repeated, his eyes wide and sightless. 'Right in front of me.'

Part Three

CHAPTER 1

THE MARSHAL HEAVED OFF his coat and placed it on the cold flags under the woman's head. She was plump and had a row of neat gray curls across her forehead. She moaned faintly, apparently more in fear than in pain. The wound seemed to be in her thigh. The Marshal took off his glasses and looked at it. There was a lot of blood but it was probably only a flesh wound or she would be in great pain.

'Signora,' said the Marshal softly, 'do you feel very much pain?'

'No . . . I can't feel anything.' She had been gazing past him, her eyes half closed, expressionless, but she suddenly opened them in alarm. 'Am I going to die?' She had seen the black shape of the priest who had followed the Marshal in and was now leaning over her.

'Nothing of the sort,' said the Marshal. 'A flesh wound in your leg, that's all. The ambulance will soon be here.'

'Put my shoes on . . . my shoes . . .' A tear rolled out of the side of the woman's eye. 'And the shopping . . .' Her hand was groping feebly about, wanting to put her world back together.

'Never mind the shopping, now. I've got your shoes here and we'll put them on in the ambulance. Do you think you could tell us what happened?'

'I don't understand . . . oh, Mother of God! What happened, what happened to me?'

'Be calm, Signora, be calm, you're going to be all right but please try and tell me . . . it came from in front so you must have seen . . . was it anybody you know?'

But the woman's shocked gaze moved rapidly from one to another of the black figures that were suddenly blocking out her normal world and she could only repeat: 'I don't understand . . .' Then she lost consciousness.

'If you're sure it's nothing serious,' said the priest, 'I'd better get back. There's the funeral . . .'

'KEEP CALM,' ordered the Marshal, opening up both the great doors and trying to push back the murmuring crowd outside. 'And stand back or the ambulance won't be able to get through!'

Inside, the woman was still unconscious, guarded by Miss White whom the Marshal had beckoned in from the Piazza.

Carabiniere Bacci had been dispatched to fetch the Captain and the Englishmen from the river where they were still working, according to the *vigile* who had come down from the bridge. They arrived after the ambulance.

'Do you know who she is?' the Captain asked, as the patient was carried out.

'The Cipriani's maid,' said the Marshal. 'I often see her shopping in the Piazza after she's taken the children to school. She usually brings the little one home from nursery school at this time, but—'

'Where was the wound?'

'In the thigh, nothing—'

'Was the child with her? Carabiniere Bacci!' He turned on the young man. 'Was the child with her?'

'I didn't see—'

'You didn't see who fired a shot under your nose, blast you!' He strode quickly into the building. The Marshal patted the boy's shoulder.

'I'm sure the child wasn't with her, sir.'

'Of course she wasn't. School closed yesterday for Christmas.'

The Piazza was empty of cars. The two *vigili* and the crowd stood waiting in silence. The ambulance turned and raced along the emptied Via Maggio toward the bridge, its siren wailing. Beyond it, the funeral cortege had finally got away and the burden of brightly-colored flowers was just visible at the far end of the cold, shadowy street where a rectangle of brilliant light indicated the river. They saw it draw in near the bridge to let the shrilling ambulance go by.

'Well . . . I think we—' The Chief turned and stopped, seeing the Marshal's streaming eyes. He had come outside without his glasses on. 'You . . . all right?'

'I'm all right, perfectly all right,' said the Marshal, catching the Chief Inspector's incredulous look as he wiped away his tears. 'It's the sunshine that does it,' he explained slowly, pointing upwards. They walked back along the passage.

Miss White had picked up the Marshal's coat and was trying to clean it with a small handkerchief. 'All this mess . . .' she said, when she saw them. Jeffreys watched the Chief's face as he took in the fur coat and running shoes. 'And who's going to clean it up?' The Cipriani's shopping lay scattered in front of the lift door next to a bag of broken green glass. There was an immense puddle of bloody water. 'It was the maid from the Cipriani's flat, wasn't it? I heard them say her name in the bar . . . Martha, she's called, a nice woman, too. She'll not be doing any cleaning for a while—there's the Cesarini's maid but we can't ask her, not her job and upsetting, too, might think she's next—and poor Signor Cipolla at the cemetery, *he* can't be expected and that leaves yours truly. Well, we're all here to help each other. You've enough to do . . . got to get on and find the murderer before we all wake up dead in our beds . . .' The monologue was the same as ever but her face was very pale and the hand that rolled and unrolled the stained handkerchief was shaking. She started to go up the stairs.

'Miss White?' called Inspector Jeffreys, then paused.

Without turning, she stopped and remarked: 'Haven't seen Signor Cesarini about today . . .'

'No, he's, as they say, helping us with our inquiries.'

She half turned now. 'Didn't want to lose my home, my little museum. It's my whole life . . . you do understand?'

'I understand.'

'I know it *did* look like him but I still couldn't swear . . . if I'd seen him from the front . . .'

'Don't worry for the moment . . . but, all the same, Miss White, if you don't mind, keep your door shut until further notice. Don't let anybody in, anybody at all.'

'But I have to—open to the public, you see.'

'Miss White, please, as a favor to me—'

'Keep the door shut. Right. Clean up this mess first—'

'Not yet. You mustn't touch anything here until the police have finished—and don't let anyone into your flat!' But she was gone.

'That's our witness, is it?' said the Chief, rolling an unlit pipe between his palms.

The Captain was coming down the stairs at a run, his hat still in his hand. 'The child's in the flat, she's all right. School finished yesterday, so—' He glanced at the Marshal. 'You knew that, of course . . .'

'But you were right to think of the child, considering where the wound was. Had she seen something?'

'Heard something—let's go inside. I have to make some phone calls.' He unlocked the flat.

'I'll stay out here,' offered Jeffreys. The Marshal had already planted his bulk outside the door. The Captain was already on the phone.

'No, no, I'll see to things out here, they don't need me in there . . .'

Jeffreys asked Carabiniere Bacci to explain the problem with Miss White who was almost sure to come down and start trying to clean everything. 'And she won't understand him—I know you could cope but you've got to make your report . . .'

The Marshal went in and stood diffidently in a corner of the dusty room, blowing his nose, while Carabiniere Bacci related his story. The boy's hands were shaking and he continually tried to hide them.

He had been on duty at the door since 9:45 A.M. The first person he had seen was the Eritrean girl who had come into the building behind him, wrapped in a green loden cloak and her white muslin veil. She had been carrying two bags of shopping and had rung for the lift. She had waited some time for it to come down as someone had just called it up, presumably Signor Cipriani who stepped out of the lift when it reached the ground floor and said 'Good morning' to Carabiniere Bacci. He was carrying his briefcase. Before the Eritrean girl could shut the lift doors, the Cipriani's maid, Martha, had come running round the corner, panting, and was in time to go up with her.

A few minutes later, Miss White had come down the staircase, she never seemed to use the lift. She had spoken vehemently and apparently encouragingly to Carabiniere Bacci, but he wasn't sure what about.

She had left the building and not returned until a few moments ago. Almost immediately, the Cipriani's maid, Martha, had come down in the lift and gone out, returning perhaps twenty minutes afterwards, with her two bags, one of groceries, the other of water.

'Did she ring for the lift?'

'Yes, sir.'

'And did it come down immediately, or was it occupied?'

'It started down immediately, sir.'

'You're positive?'

'Yes, sir.'

'And it was empty when it arrived?'

'Yes . . .'

'You're not sure. Did you look?'

'Yes, sir.'

'Well, then?'

'I looked, sir, but if someone were in there and crouch-ing . . .'

It was true. The window in the outer door of the lift was narrow and at eye-level. The maid's key had been still in the door. The Captain had opened it. The windows of the inner double doors were larger, but again they stopped before waist level so that anybody crouching . . .

'Did she open the doors?'

'The outer one, yes, but then she . . .'

'She what?'

'She didn't get in immediately . . . she bent forward a little.

'Bent forward? How? Why?'

'I'm not sure, sir, but I don't think she'd opened the inner doors when the shot was fired.'

'You said she had two shopping bags,' put in the Marshal from his corner.

'Yes, sir.'

'So she must have put at least one of them down to find her key and unlock the lift door.'

'Yes, I suppose she must, sir . . . Only, once the lift had come down empty, I more or less . . .' The unfortunate Carabiniere blushed deeply.

'Stopped looking,' finished the Marshal blandly. 'Never stop looking, Carabiniere Bacci. She bent down, in all likelihood, to pick up her shopping after unlocking the door, because the inner doors can simply be pushed open; they swing inwards.'

'Yes, sir.'

'But her key is still in the lock,' said the Marshal, more blandly than ever.

'Sir?'

'Her key, Carabiniere Bacci, is still in the lock. She would take it out first, wouldn't she, before picking up her shopping and stepping into the lift?'

'I . . . yes . . .'

'It doesn't do to lose sight of plain everyday facts,' murmured the Marshal. He fished out a large handkerchief and turned away to blow his nose protractedly.

'Are you sure she did bend down?' asked the Captain.

'I . . . it was just an impression I had, sir, out of the corner of my eye . . . but then immediately there was the shot and she fell.'

'Did you look inside the lift straight away?'

'I—no, sir, I looked at the woman to see if—'

'Did you look in the lift at all?'

'No, sir,' he whispered. 'But I was standing in front of it by then so nobody could have got out.'

'But they could have gone back up?'

'No, sir, they couldn't, because the outer door was still open. The lift won't work with the outer door open.'

And the Marshal had arrived immediately after that.

'You didn't see anybody?' The Captain turned to the Marshal's corner.

'There was nobody there, sir,' His hands were burrowing in his pockets, seeking his dark glasses.

'Well, we can check on all the tenants, but it's beginning to sound as if this wretched woman shot herself, by accident, of course—she could have been carrying the gun for someone else . . . Well, her clothing will be searched at the hospital, and as soon as the doctors will allow it, a paraffin test. . . is there something wrong, Marshal?'

'No, sir, no . . . nothing . . . As a matter of fact, if you don't really need me here I have some things to see to in my office . . .' He was moving, almost imperceptibly, toward the door.

'I see,' said the Captain with chilling politeness. 'No doubt you are concerned to get your paperwork in order. Going home for Christmas, I imagine.'

The Marshal mumbled some incomprehensible words of assent.

'By all means, then. As there's nothing much you can do here.'

'I'll take Carabiniere Bacci with me—you'll be wanting a written report from him, I expect. He may need a bit of help . . .'

'I imagine so. I'd like the report on my desk before two. I have a meeting with the Substitute Prosecutor at three.'

'At three . . . you might put him off for an hour or so . . . under the circumstances . . .'

'I might. But I want that report on my desk at two.'

'At two. Carabiniere Bacci . . .' They left in silence. The Chief Inspector stared after them, unsure what was going on.

There was no time for speculation. Immediately after their departure, Jeffreys opened the door again. Dr Biondini had brought two of his custodians over from the Palatine gallery to remove the majolica bust and there were sheaves of papers for the Captain to sign. It was one less headache for the Captain but Biondini seemed harassed.

'I'll be dealing with paperwork over this business for a year . . .'

They were still packing the bust when the technicians arrived.

'Can we plug the lights in in here? We'll take all this stuff away with us . . .'

The Captain tried to give them instructions while dealing with the over-anxious Biondini.

'Where do I sign? Surely we've done this one twice already?'

'Yes, it has to be in triplicate . . . and here . . . leave that, I'll fill in the dates later . . .'

'Captain?' Jeffreys looked in again. 'I think this lady . . .'

'Please excuse me, I just wanted to ask something.'

Seeing Signora Cipriani hovering behind Jeffreys, the Captain thrust the papers at Biondini and went to the door.

'The child . . . ?'

'She's here with me . . . you said not to leave her alone, so . . . It's just that I was wondering if it was all right for me to go to the hospital once Vincenzo gets home . . . after lunch. Poor Martha—'

'No. I'd rather you stayed in the building until I'm certain there's no further danger—and don't open your door to anyone.'

'Yes, of course. Poor Martha, and at Christmas . . . her daughter is arriving today . . . I wanted to offer . . .'

'Yes, I understand, but I must ask you to stay here for the moment. I'll let you know as soon as I can—and do keep the little girl with you.' Giovanna was hovering in the open doorway of the lift where she had evidently been told to stay. Every now and then she peeped out and threatened Jeffreys with a pink water-pistol. The Captain watched them shut themselves in the lift and go up, then turned to the technicians. 'I know it's a lot to ask but if you could get me something on paper, however tentative, by this afternoon . . . I have to see the S.P. at three unless I can put him off . . .'

THE MARSHAL was brooding in his office chair. A copy of Carabiniere Bacci's report on the finding of the body was before him on the desk. Carabiniere Bacci stood beside him. His coat was unbuttoned but the Marshal had said, without looking up, 'Don't take it off,' and had gone on brooding over the report. At last he sighed and sank back a little in his chair. 'You're going to have to write this report again.'

'Sir . . . ?'

'Write it again. Accurately.'

'Yes, sir . . . But the Captain was with me when—'

'The Captain,unfortunately, was not with you when you first went to Via Maggio, otherwise . . .'

'But I thought . . . they said that Cesarini—'

'Is helping the Captain with his inquiries. But he didn't kill the Englishman and he probably doesn't know who did. Only you know that.'

Suddenly, Carabiniere Bacci's pale face turned red. He began to shake.

The Marshal turned his great eyes on him sadly. 'Bring me Cipolla. He should be back from the cemetery by now.'

'Cipolla . . .'

'The cleaner.'

'Yes, sir.'

'We're going to take his statement again, you and I together. He was very frightened, Carabiniere Bacci.'

'Yes, sir.' He was whispering, his throat too dry to speak.

'He wanted me. I was ill, it's true, but I admit I was glad to be out of it . . . not to be the one . . . I'm not competent . . . and he was frightened of you, of the Captain. Bring him to me, Carabiniere Bacci, and apologize for doing it on the day of the funeral. Tell him I'm here and I'm waiting for him. That he can tell me.'

'Yes, sir,' whispered Carabiniere Bacci.

THE CHIEF had watched Jeffreys fight off his exhaustion and, having seen him succeed, suggested that they go off for lunch and a rest.

'D'you know what I'd like more than anything, Jeffreys? I'd like a beer. Do you think there's any chance of getting one?'

'Easily.' They were crossing the river in a squad car. 'I'll ask him to drop us at the bar near the Christmas trees, then we're only two minutes from the vicarage.'

'And Felicity's shepherd's pie.'

'Exactly.' Neither would ever have believed that they could be on such friendly terms. Each had seen the other hard-pressed, the Chief morally, Jeffreys physically, and found they had a fighting spirit in common. Now they were both feeling very English and very homesick. The idea of getting in a quick beer before lunch had a familiar appeal.

The barman was standing on a little stool unhooking one of the blue and silver boxes containing Christmas cakes which hung in clusters from the ceiling.

A bus driver was drinking a glass of red wine in the far corner and recounting a story heatedly to three listeners. He had a small dressing on his forehead.

'Isn't that the driver . . . ?' The Chief was looking hard at him.

'Yes, I'm sure it is.' Jeffreys tried to catch what he was saying.

'. . . Well, you know how narrow it gets once you pass the junction . . . hardly room for two people to walk—the bus is a write-off, I reckon.'

'Did you hit the windscreen?'

'I may have done, it's difficult to remember . . .' In fact, he had fainted after being rescued and had banged his head on a Carabiniere car wing-mirror. 'Nor would you with a gun in your back . . .' He broke off, realizing that he had seen the two Englishmen who were staring at him last night at the police station. He turned away and continued in more sub-dued tones.

'Feeling better, Jeffreys?'

'Much better.'

'Shepherd's pie, then, if we're not too late.'

Walking down to the vicarage, they agreed to ring the Consulate and see if there was any chance of a plane home. If the case was going to drag on they had every excuse for going home for Christmas and reporting on the changed state of affairs in the case.

'All the same,' said the Chief, as they waited for the vicar to answer the bell, 'I wouldn't have minded a word with that fat chap we saw this morning. He looked to me like someone who knew something he wasn't telling.'

And the Captain, standing at the window in his office, waiting for the results of the search and the paraffin test that were being carried out in the emergency hospital of San Giovanni di Dio next door, waiting for something, anything, that might placate an irritable Substitute Prosecutor at three o'clock, was beginning to think the same thing.

THE MARSHAL stood up when he heard the door opening. 'Leave your coats here and come through to my quarters where we won't be disturbed.' He led the way, taking them right through into the kitchen. He sat them down at the little kitchen table, took a bottle of *vinsanto* from a painted cupboard on the wall and set three glasses out. When he had filled them he sat down heavily on his own straight-backed chair and drank his *vinsanto* off delicately, in one draft, forgetting the doctor's advice completely. He placed his hands squarely on his knees and spoke softly to the table: 'We don't. . . we don't want anyone else to get hurt . . . and there's something I don't know . . .' He tailed off and then looked up, fixing the little man with his great rolling eyes. The cleaner gazed back at him with his permanent expression of humble surprise beneath the spiky black hair. 'Tell me now, Cipolla, before you tell me anything else . . . what did you do with the gun?'

CHAPTER 2

'I THREW IT INTO the courtyard, Marshal.'

'Why?'

'I suppose I was frightened.'

'Were you trying to hide it?'

'I don't think so . . . I only threw it just outside the french window. I just wanted to get it away from me. I was going to give it to you when you came, but . . .'

'But I didn't come.'

'No.' The little cleaner glanced worriedly at Carabiniere Bacci, not wanting to offend.

'But I did come later.'

'Yes, Marshal, but I'd been sent outside . . .'

'Why didn't you ask to come in?'

The cleaner looked at him uncomprehendingly. The idea that he should have interrupted officers, professors, experts, photographers . . . when he'd been told to go and stay out of the way in the courtyard . . . he couldn't even understand the question. The Marshal left it and went on.

'So what happened to the gun then?'

'I picked it up, Marshal.'

'Out there, in front of the window, while we were inside?'

'Yes.'

'Did you pick it up to conceal it somewhere?'

'Conceal it?'

'Yes, hide it?'

'But . . . no. I picked it up because I was tidying the

courtyard . . . he told me to . . .' Another apprehensive glance at Carabiniere Bacci.

'I see. So you tidied up. What else did you pick up?'

'The usual things. Clothes-pegs, mostly, and a sock and two handkerchiefs dropped from somebody's washing line. And a toy gun, pink plastic . . . but I couldn't sweep up like I usually do because . . .'

'Because you didn't have your brush,' finished the Marshal, remembering his dream. The familiar figure of Cipolla always had a brush and bucket slung over his right shoulder. 'And what did you do with all this stuff you picked up?'

'Put it in a polythene bag, as usual, and then I waited for you to come out so I could give it to you.'

'But you didn't give it to me, Cipolla.'

'No, Marshal . . .'

'Why not?'

'You told me to put it down,' he whispered, 'and come with you to the station . . .'

'But you could have *said*, surely, to me?'

'Yes . . . but I was . . . the others were there . . . so I just did what you told me. I thought it didn't matter anyway . . .'

'Didn't *matter*?'

'About telling you just then. I thought you were arresting me.'

'You thought. . . ? What, the whole time? Even in the bar?'

'Yes.'

'Have you ever *been* arrested, Cipolla?'

'No, Marshal!' His face reddened.

'No, I don't suppose you have. So, you put the bag containing the gun down in the entrance hall?'

'By the lift door, Marshal. I always put it there so that people can collect their things and some clothes-pegs—everybody drops those and nobody has a key to the courtyard except the Cesarini. There's a little hook by the lift door. I always leave the bag there.'

'And didn't you worry afterwards about what would happen if the gun were left there like that?'

'Is that what happened to that poor woman? But I thought—there were so many policemen there searching—I thought they'd have found it.'

So they would have done, but it hadn't been there when they searched the entrance and when they got to the courtyard he had hung it on its hook in the hall. Nobody, in the meantime, had taken the slightest notice of the little cleaner.

'Well, Carabiniere Bacci?' The Marshal rolled his eyes round and settled his gaze on the young man who had begun by being rigid and red in the face and was now pale and drawn.

'Yes, sir.'

'Is that what she was bending over to do?'

'Yes, sir, I realize now . . .'

'Oh, you do?'

'It's just that I wasn't actually watching her, sir. But now I remember the noise . . . she must have been feeling in the bag.'

'Clothes-pegs?'

'Yes, sir, I remember the rattling now.'

'Go and find the gun, Carabiniere Bacci.'

'Yes, sir.'

'And try not to shoot yourself.'

'Yes, sir.' He got up abruptly and went out.

The Marshal sighed and rubbed a weary hand over his face. He kept his hand there and his eyes closed for a while, not wanting to start. Then, in silence, he refilled their glasses.

The little cleaner didn't speak but accepted the drink passively.

He looks so calm, thought the Marshal. Ever since it happened, he's looked so calm . . . But then he remembered Cipolla as he used to be, trotting rapidly across the Piazza in his black smock, hair on end, bucket and brush slung over his shoulder. Dodging about the city among the big palaces, nodding to friends, acquaintances, employers, sweeping his way down staircases, rubbing industriously at great brass doorknobs, polishing a plate glass window which might contain one article of clothing with a price tag equal to his year's salary . . . this calmness wasn't real . . .

There was something about the image of Cipolla's old self that put the Marshal in mind of the little English lady, living alone, tripping across the Piazza trying to carry those picture frames . . . People on the fringes of life, never really included. Even as a murderer Cipolla hadn't made an impression, everybody had ignored him as they always had. The meek don't inherit much in a country where you have to be a genius to survive, let alone get anywhere. The Marshal felt tired. He would have liked to send the little cleaner about his business, ignore him like everyone else had done, and take himself off to bed. But tomorrow was Christmas and a twenty-hour train journey lay before him, and the cleaner's hollow eyes were watching him, patiently, humbly, waiting for the Marshal to do something about him, knowing nobody else would. Each time . . . directly after the murder, that few seconds in the entrance hall when Cipolla had held the gun in a polythene bag under their noses, then in the blocked funeral car . . . that white face, the humble, hopeful eyes . . . had he only meant to wait until after the funeral and then, if the Marshal still hadn't come for him . . . ?

'What were you going to do, Cipolla? Tonight, once your sister and brother-in-law had left?'

Cipolla lowered his eyes without answering, like a child caught on the point of stealing jam. All his reactions seemed to be on a child-like level, an imitation of the adult response, not fully developed. Was that perhaps why everyone ignored him when anything serious was afoot? As if they told him, 'Go out and find something to do, stay out of the room while the grown-ups talk.' It could also have a lot to do with his being so tiny. Had he felt like an adult when, for a few seconds, he'd held a gun in his hand and fired? Or had that been an imitation too, the man's death more or less an accident? To be followed by a child's attempt at suicide which might or might not succeed . . . probably not, depending on what . . .

'What was it to be, Cipolla, the river? The bell tower?'

Giotto's marble *campanile* was used quite frequently by suicides who were past caring about anyone who might be walking or driving in the busy square below.

'Not the *campanile*,' whispered Cipolla, still with lowered eyes. 'I read in the *Nazione* about that old man . . .'

A man of eighty-four who had left a note saying he was exhausted with the struggle of trying to exist on a pitiful amount of money which was hardly enough to feed his little black and white dog. He had jumped from the bell tower and crashed through the windscreen of a car, killing not only himself but the young girl who was driving. No one had thought of the dog until neighbors heard it whimpering two days later. There was no food in the house.

'I didn't want to hurt anyone. I've done enough harm already.'

'The river then?' No answer. So it was to have been the river. 'And you're what? Forty-two years old?'

'Yes, Marshal.' He was sitting very still and upright. The

unruly hair accentuated the impression of a schoolboy. It was impossible not to think of Cipolla as the Englishman's victim. But the Englishman was dead and Cipolla was not, and the Marshal had a job to do, though he had never liked it less.

'How old were you during the war?' he asked suddenly.

'About six when it finished.'

'Can you remember much about it?' He shouldn't be asking these questions, and yet, it was a way of giving him some attention.

'Only bits, mostly toward the end when we had to leave. Our house was bombed.'

'Couldn't you find shelter in the city anywhere?'

'My mother thought we'd be safer in the country . . . she had a sister who lived further north, near Rome. She said there'd be food there, that there was always food in the country.'

'And was there?'

'No. For a long time we used to collect wild beet and fennel and nettles and boil them.'

'Bread?'

'For a while, until the flour ran out.'

'How many were you?'

'Four, including my mother.'

'And your aunt?'

'We never found her. The cottage had been bombed. Part of it was still standing and had been used by soldiers. The furniture had been used for firewood and there was a large hole in the roof. We lived in the barn until the planes came.'

'Which planes?'

'Every sort. English, German, American. They flew low and fired at anything that moved. I suppose there must have been soldiers about but we never saw any. There was bombing, too. I remember a lot of fires.'

'Did you know which side you were on?'

'Which side . . . ?'

'The planes that came over, did you know which side you were on in the war?'

'I don't think so . . . my mother used to curse all of them, Italians too, for trying to murder her children. I only knew I had to hide and keep still if I heard planes. I knew I was hungry.'

'What happened next, when you left the barn?'

'I'm not sure. A lot of moving about. We ended up in Rome because my mother said her sister must have gone there along with all the other refugees whose farms were ruined. I suppose she must have been killed but I can't remember whether we ever found out . . . I don't know how we lived in Rome but eventually we went back to the country where my mother and my brother and sister worked on a farm. I was the youngest . . .'

'I didn't see your brother at the funeral?'

'No, he emigrated to America as soon as he could, that is, as soon as I was old enough to work too.'

'Did you like farm work?'

'No, I hated it. I hated the country.'

No wonder. After his first experience of it. Boiled nettles and strafing aeroplanes.

'How old were you when you first came to Florence?'

'Fourteen, a little more.'

'And you came alone?'

'Yes. It was the first time I'd ever been anywhere by train.'

'Did your father . . . you had a father?'

'He was killed in Greece.'

'Go on. Tell me about coming to Florence. Where did you stay?'

'In a hostel. The priest at home arranged it for me. I

started by doing some cleaning work in a church here, but I soon found plenty more work and, eventually, a cheap flat in Via Romana.'

'And then you got married?'

'Not then, later. First my mother died and my sister came up here to live with me. She got a job in a *trattoria* run by some people we knew from Salerno. Then when she married Bellini she had her own home next to you . . .'

The Marshal glanced at a white bowl with a plate on it standing on the refrigerator.

'And then you married?'

'Yes.' A strange look came over his face as they approached the present. Sooner or later, he must break down . . . better here than among strangers at Headquarters . . . even so, it might be wiser to wait until Carabiniere Bacci—and where the devil was he anyway? The Marshal filled their glasses.

'Drink it up,' he said, watching him. How different would Cipolla have been if he'd had food when he needed it? If he'd grown to a normal man's size? It was useless to speculate. And there were thousands like him.

'Who insures you? You work for so many people all over town.'

'Nobody . . . I've got a small policy and we try . . . and we tried to save a little. We had no children, you see, so— Milena couldn't—'

'So you both worked and saved . . . ?'

'No, no . . . it wasn't like that . . .' He began to talk faster, loosing his hands from his lap to accentuate, to explain.

It may be, thought the Marshal, that he's never really talked to anybody about himself in his life . . . or else it's the *vinsanto*. It was true that his face was a little pink.

'It wasn't like that. I didn't want her to have to work. My mother killed herself working to bring us up alone . . . And

then, what could she have done? Cleaning like me? She only
had elementary education. And she had no children. It's one
thing to do unpleasant work when you've got the pleasure of
children to buy for, there's some point in that, but for her to
do that sort of work and only me to come home to . . .
Besides, I thought it would be good for her to live like a
"Signora," be a bit special . . . Other women, you see, sometimes upset her—it wasn't that they meant to, I suppose they
couldn't help it . . .'

'Those with children, you mean?'

'Yes . . . Even my sister—they didn't mean to . . . She used
to cry in the night when she thought I was asleep. I always
knew why.'

'She wasn't bored at home?'

'Bored . . . ? I don't think . . . I suggested she should take
her Middle School Certificate—it only takes a year and lots
of people like us do it now, at night school, but she wouldn't
go. She was afraid of people knowing and thinking it ridiculous at her age . . . In the end I talked her into having some
English lessons from Miss White. Nobody else needed to
know and I thought it might take her mind off things, but it
was no good . . . Miss White is very *simpatica*, very patient,
but she doesn't speak any Italian and Milena didn't know a
word of English, so . . .'

'More tears?'

'Yes.'

The Marshal thought he was beginning to understand.
Surely Milena had only agreed to play the 'Signora' to please
him? What pleasure could she have in sitting at home alone
when all her neighbors either had children or worked or,
more probably, both. It wasn't unusual; couples spent their
lives doing a job or living in a place, thinking they were
pleasing each other, never admitting how they hated it . . .

What if that was what he was doing himself? For whose benefit was he a thousand miles away from his family? Would his wife really worry about the children having to change schools, or his mother be so upset about leaving her home village for the first time in her life? Or did they all imagine that he liked leading a bachelor life up here, since he always tried to hide the fact that he was desperately lonely without them? He made up his mind to sort it out this holiday. But just now he shouldn't be thinking about himself.

'So all this time you were working hard and keeping both of you. It must have meant long hours . . . it's not well-paid work.'

'No, but I don't mind long hours. I enjoy work, I like to go about the city, it suits me.'

Naturally. No danger of open fields and planes, no nettle soup. He liked to trot in the shadow of huge buildings that had stood for five hundred years and more, surrounded by shops bulging with food! But mightn't his wife have liked it, too?

'Your wife did go out to work at one time, didn't she?' They had to come to it some time.

'That was after we found out about . . . the illness.'

'She went to work when she was *ill*?'

'We had no choice, in the end . . . the policy covered the operation but then I had to be off work . . . My sister did what she could, but with children to look after as well . . . Anyway, I lost some wages and we got a bit behind—I got everything straight in the end but there was nothing left . . . nothing for . . . and we knew . . .'

They knew she was going to die and that too costs money.

'The one thing she didn't want was to die in a hospital. A month or so after the operation she felt more or less normal again—they hadn't done anything, you see . . . they couldn't—she said she wanted to look for a little job, if only for a few weeks so that I would be able to afford to stay at home with her when . . .'

So, in the end, she had escaped from the four walls, however briefly.

Cipolla's face was very red. Perhaps the *vinsanto* . . .

'When did you last eat?' asked the Marshal abruptly.

'I can't remember.'

'Today or yesterday?'

'I . . . yesterday . . . I don't know . . . it might have been the day before . . .'

The Marshal heaved his great bulk away from the table and took the white bowl from the refrigerator.

'I couldn't take your meal, Marshal.'

'I've eaten,' lied the Marshal. 'Before you arrived. And it was your sister who made this so I can't see any good reason why you shouldn't have some of it.'

'Is she . . . will you . . . ?'

'I'll go round there later.'

When Carabiniere Bacci tapped gently on the door and came in, he was astonished to see the Marshal stirring a steaming pan of soup and the little cleaner sitting obediently at the table with a striped bowl and a plate before him. There was a second place set beside him.

'Marshal? They'd already taken the bag away so I had to—'

'Sit down,' interrupted the Marshal, and began ladling soup into their bowls as though he were feeding his own children. 'And when did you last eat? Eh?' he growled at the stunned Carabiniere Bacci.

'Last night, sir . . .'

'Well then. Eat, go on.' He began sawing enormous chunks of bread for them from a rough, floury loaf. 'Here you are. Bread. Eat it.' And he sat down, satisfied, to watch them.

'After the gun, Marshal—they'd already found the hole burnt in the bag and traces of powder on everything inside, but the gun isn't there, so—'

'Later.'

When they had finished, the Marshal took their plates away and put them in the sink. The kitchen window had patches of steam in the center of each pane. Around the edges he glimpsed the winter sun shining on the head of a Roman statue and the top of a laurel hedge where the Boboli Gardens began. He came back and sat down.

'Do you mind very much, Cipolla, if Carabiniere Bacci stays with us? He's a good lad, a serious lad.'

'I can see that, Marshal. And he's young and has to learn his job . . . I've caused you all a lot of trouble . . .'

Was he even pleased to have an audience, for once in his life? Even so, he was too calm . . .

'So . . . you needed the money because of her illness. How did she come to work for the Englishman?'

'It was difficult to find anything. These days, it's not like when I started . . . and most people want somebody permanent. She couldn't lie about it. In the end I thought of something I'd tried before—I'd written to the heads of all the condominiums I worked for and asked them if I could clean their courtyards once a month as well as doing the stairs weekly—that's how I got straight when we were behind. So I asked each of my employers if they knew of any one-off jobs or temporary work.'

'And you asked the Englishman?'

'No, no, I didn't know him, though I'd seen him, of course. I asked Signor Cesarini because he's the head of that condominium and in charge of my work. At first he said no but then he changed his mind. He told me that the Englishman's flat needed cleaning up, that it was his property and he was disgusted by the state it was in. He said the whole place needed cleaning out but that it had to be done within about three weeks which meant full-time work just for that period. It was just what we wanted.'

'So the Signora went to work. Did she like it?'

'She didn't seem unhappy. It was dirty work, though, the whole place was so filthy, she said, it mustn't have been touched for years. Even so, it was a relief not to have to worry about the money business, to know that I'd be with her when . . .

'Sometimes we used to have breakfast together in the bar—a thing I've never done, but we had to one morning because we were a bit late, she hadn't felt well in the night— she enjoyed it so much that I thought we should do it as much as possible. She liked me to collect her, too, in the evenings, so I changed my round and did this end last so that we could walk home together.'

'Did your wife have a key to the Englishman's flat?'

'No, never. He would get up and let her in himself and then go back to bed. Some people are like that; they don't trust anybody. Sometimes he would get up later and go out.'

'He never objected to her coming? After all, it wasn't his idea.'

'No . . . he just ignored her . . . Signor Cesarini had told her what to do, to clean the floors and windows, the kitchen and bathroom, but not to touch the living-room furniture or ever go in the bedroom. He used to lock the bedroom door when he went out, the Englishman, I mean.'

'And he always ignored her? He never . . .' The Marshal hesitated, but the question had to be asked and it was better broached by him.

'He never bothered your wife . . . tried to—'

'No!' Cipolla blushed. 'Nothing like that—he never spoke to her! Never anything—'

'All right, it's all right. I had to ask you because other people will.' The Marshal watched his face closely. 'Because if that were the case things would go easy with you, very easy indeed . . . a crime of passion . . .'

'But that's not what happened.' Not a flicker of guile in his face.

'All right. Just understand that that's the reason I had to ask, and why others will ask. It's no reflection on your wife. Now tell me what did happen.'

'He didn't pay her.'

'What, never?'

'No. We expected him to pay each week at first but he always happened to be out on the Friday when she finished work. We began to get worried—mainly because Milena had found unpaid bills all over the house when she was cleaning. We talked it over and I decided to go and see Signor Cesarini. He laughed and said the Englishman was an old miser but he would probably pay up in the end.'

'Probably?'

'Yes. I told him we needed the money, that we had bills to pay—I didn't feel I could tell him the real reason, maybe I should have done but I couldn't—and he laughed again and slapped my shoulder. He said, "Nobody pays bills in Italy! Forget it, enjoy yourself!" Milena decided to try asking the Englishman, although she wasn't even sure whether he understood Italian.'

'And did he?'

'Oh yes. He spoke with a strange accent but even so . . . he asked her. "Did I arrange for you to work here?" "Not you exactly, but—" "Who arranged it?" "Signor Cesarini." "So he'll pay you, not me. I have nothing to do with it." He told her to get out if she didn't want to do the work, that he didn't care either way and that if she made a nuisance of herself he would call the police and accuse her of having stolen from him, of being in his house without his permission, that Cesarini would back him up. When she still didn't leave he threatened her with the gun he kept on his desk.'

'Wasn't she afraid of him?'

'In her condition, why should she be?'

'And you?'

Cipolla lowered his head. 'He was a very big man. On her last day of work Milena decided that she wouldn't leave without her money no matter what he threatened. After all, she had nothing to lose. But when she got there he was out—or just not answering the door. She went back day after day but she could never get in and then eventually the illness began to take hold . . .'

'How did you manage?'

'I was at my wits' end. My sister gave me what she could and she came down and prepared some food for us each morning, then rushed back to see to the children. Neighbors came in, too. But it tired her to have people there she had to talk to, she needed me. She needed me and I couldn't be there . . . Do you know how much morphine costs? I don't understand how these drug addicts . . . And I'd promised to be with her, I'd promised . . .'

The low red sun was glowing outside the kitchen window but the light was already failing. A group of children, probably including Cipolla's nephews and nieces, were playing under the window in the wilderness that the Marshal called his garden and which he would never allow his baffled neighbor to tidy up for him. The children played there every day and the Marshal pretended not to see them. If he wanted peace and quiet he would let himself be seen, from the back, at the window and they would flee. Then he would be full of remorse for ten minutes until they returned. He stood up now and gave them a glimpse of his black jacket and braided collar, afraid their cheerful noise might distress the little cleaner.

'The Marshal's in! Scram!' They skidded away like frightened rabbits.

'Tell me about that night.'

Cipolla's thin hands turned round and round on themselves in his lap.

'My sister was there. Milena had been very depressed but during that last week somehow . . . maybe it was the morphine . . . she slept most of the time . . . Not a natural sleep, her eyes would be half open and she would snore, Milena never . . . but when she was awake she seemed to have forgotten what was happening to her and she would talk about what she would do when she was up and about—it was worse than when she'd been depressed . . . I shouldn't say that, it must have been better for her. That night, around midnight, she was awake and she seemed feverish, excitable. She asked my sister for a mirror. Her hair had gone completely gray in the last month or so but I don't think she'd seen it . . . Still, we couldn't refuse.'

' "How ugly I am," she said, when she saw herself, "I think I'll have my hair done as soon as I'm better—I can afford it now I've got a job, you know. What would you say if I were to go blonde? I get bored, do you know that?" Then she began asking for her mother. Her mother had died when Milena was thirteen so we realized . . . my sister put her coat on and ran up for the priest . . .

'After the Sacrament she was much quieter. She only spoke once more before . . . I'm not sure what she said.

'When the women came they sent me into the other room. One of them had brought some grappa for me, though I don't normally drink.

'It seemed to take a long time . . . the room was so silent and I felt as if I were choking. After a while I slipped out.'

'Can you remember where you went?'

'I think so . . . I crossed the Ponte Vecchio and wandered about in the center, looking at the Christmas lights.'

'Were you thinking about Christmas?'

'No. It was just something to fix on . . . I came back across the Santa Trinita, I stopped there for a minute . . .'

'Were you thinking of the river even then?'

His face flushed and his eyes left the Marshal's. 'No . . . that was after . . . no.'

'Did you intend to go and see the Englishman?'

'No, not at all, it just happened. I came back down Via Maggio, I was thinking about the money then . . . but just as I came to the door of number fifty-eight, it opened.'

'Did you see anyone?'

'No . . . at least, I think the guard may have been on the street. I think I saw him go into one of the houses but the street isn't that well lit . . . no one else. When I saw the door spring open I walked in . . . I don't know what I was going to do. It was too late for the money, but even so, he should have paid her . . . I closed the door.'

'Did you ring the bell?'

'No. The flat door opened in front of me, too, as if he were expecting me. It didn't seem strange then—Will anyone believe me?'

'They'll believe you. He was expecting someone, not you.'

'Then that's why . . . I went in and shut the door. He was walking away from it as if he'd just opened it. When he turned round and saw me I suppose he got a fright. He looked horrified and he began talking rapidly in English. I began demanding Milena's money. He tried to push me out of the door, telling me to get out, in Italian, and even picking up the gun.'

'Were you afraid he'd use it?'

'I don't think so.' Something didn't ring true, it was out of character, even in those circumstances.

'What did you do?'

'I refused to leave. I said he could call the police if he wanted to—I think I said I knew you. His face was livid. He dropped the gun on a chair and got hold of me . . .'

'He hit you?'

'He slapped me,' whispered Cipolla. 'In the face, as if I were a child. He said my wife was a thief and had stolen things while he was out, that he had told everyone in the Piazza, he . . . he . . . I must have been facing the bedroom, then. The door was open and the light on. He suddenly let go of me and rushed to the bedroom door as if he had forgotten me—'

'The safe,' murmured the Marshal. 'It was open; he was afraid you'd see it.'

'I didn't see anything . . . I didn't know . . . I picked up the gun, then, from the chair. I didn't know how to use it but I wanted to do something, something to make him take notice. I pointed it toward the bedroom door as he was going through. I shut my eyes and waited. Then I fired it. I fired it . . .'

'But he hadn't gone through?'

'No. I don't understand what happened. I didn't expect him to be there when I fired. When I opened my eyes, he was there for a second, holding the door handle . . .'

'He was closing it . . .'

'Perhaps. Then he fell.'

'What did you do?'

'Nothing immediately. I stood where I was. I heard someone at the door, I'm sure.'

'One person?'

'I think so . . . very soft steps in the passageway, then going up the stairs, then . . .'

'Then you went into the bathroom and you were sick.' The little man jumped. The one thing he hadn't wanted to tell. 'And you were sick at the bridge, too. How much of the grappa did you drink?'

'I can't remember. I don't know how much was in the bottle. It's just that I don't drink, I'm not used . . . Will you have to tell people?'

'Yes. But they'll realize you didn't mean to get drunk. After all, it was someone else who gave you the stuff and you weren't in any condition to watch what you were doing.' And it was the only thing that accounted for his attempt to argue with the bigger man. 'So you decided to ring me? It must still have been very early in the morning?'

'It was four o'clock, there was a clock there on the desk. I sat down to wait for a reasonable hour.'

'You sat down . . . ? You didn't think of calling a doctor? What if—'

'Oh no,' said the little man quietly. 'Oh no, because he was dead . . .' His vacant eyes were dilated. 'Oh no. His eyes were open, I looked. And his teeth came out. His teeth . . . oh no, oh no . . . ! 'His head was going back.

'Hold him!' The Marshal jumped to his feet but Carabiniere Bacci was quicker. The frail body was rattling as though some unseen hand were shaking the little man in rage. His breath came in deep noisy groans.

'Get some water.' The Marshal was holding him now, telling him over and over, 'Let it go, man, let it go . . .'

Cipolla kept his dilated eyes fixed on the Marshal as the fit rattled him. Suddenly the eyes narrowed until they were almost invisible and he found his voice, high-pitched and grating, but his own voice.

'What have I done? Oh, Marshal, what have I done?'

'The water, sir.'

'Here, drink this, and take your time.'

'WHAT WILL happen to him?' whispered Carabiniere Bacci. He had brought their coats through. Cipolla was in the bathroom, for the Marshal had insisted that he wash and shave before they left.

'He'll go to the Murate,' growled the Marshal, 'what do you expect? You wanted a murderer and now you've got one. He probably doesn't live up to your expectations but there he is. As for what will happen to him—what happened to my perfect student? Articles 62, 62 bis of your Penal Code. Read them again, they might mean something to you now.'

'Yes, sir.'

'And pull yourself together, Carabiniere! We've still got work to do.'

'Yes, sir.' Carabiniere Bacci, white-faced and dark-eyed, tried to straighten his crumpled, dusty uniform.

'Look after the phone while we're gone.' The Marshal buttoned up his greatcoat and paused to say quietly, 'Don't worry. It's just possible that the verdict could be accidental death. And when he comes out I'm here to help him. When all's said and done, we're all Italians . . . even we Sicilians, eh?'

'Yes, sir . . . but . . . will they believe him?'

'Do you?'

CHAPTER 3

'WELL, THEY PULLED THAT one out of a hat,' remarked
the Chief Inspector, as the river, pink and dark purple with
the last of the sunset, dropped away below them. Dots of light
were appearing here and there in the dusk.

'Do you think the family will pursue it?'

'I very much doubt it.' On their last visit to the Captain's
office they had been informed that Langley-Smythe's family
were entitled to bring a civil action when the case came to
court, but that, since the accused was not in a position to pay
damages, it would only serve to draw attention . . .

The couple of servants involved in the villa robberies had
already been found and were talking. The Chief had not
been able, of course, to speak for the family but he could say
he thought it unlikely . . .

The nice, red-haired girl from the Consulate had turned
up with some papers concerning the body which had to be
signed. She also brought a folder with two airline tickets.

'We thought you'd want to get home tonight with it being
Christmas Eve. The scheduled flight's left, I'm afraid: this is
a charter that will land you at Luton, but they should provide
a bus at the other end. The body will go on the scheduled
flight the day after tomorrow.' When she was closing her
briefcase, Jeffreys managed to move in on her:

'I'm glad we met you.'

'Why's that?' She smiled.

'Because otherwise I'd have come to the conclusion that
all the English people living here were a bit . . .'

'Dotty? Give me another ten years or so, I've only been here two.'

'*Are* they all dotty?'

'No, no. It's just the ones who stick together, the "colony." They're rather noticeable. There are hundreds of English people working and studying here who just blend in.'

'You blend in very nicely. Is this your scarf?'

'Thanks.'

'If you weren't packing us off on a plane I'd ask you what you were doing tonight.'

'And I'd tell you I was going to the Mayor's reception. If you weren't going off on a plane you could come.'

'I'll be back—to check up on whether you're going dotty.'

'Signorina.' The Captain came forward to shake her hand with a solemn little bow that brought the faintest flush to the girl's face. The Captain, in Jeffreys's opinion, held that hand at least a second longer than was absolutely necessary, and when the Lieutenant who came to escort her out flicked back his sword and bowed too, and the two of them went off chatting amiably in Italian, Jeffreys muttered, 'Smoothies.' And he hadn't even had chance to get a look at an Italian girl. He had, however, found a chance to telephone Carabiniere Bacci at Pitti before they left to tell him:

'About that gun . . . I think you should talk to the little girl with the pink water-pistol . . .'

'Do you know,' mused the Chief, as they unfastened their safety-belts, 'I might try Florence for a holiday sometime. I think my wife would like the shops.'

'You didn't find the food too bad, then?'

'No . . .' conceded the Chief generously, 'I can't really say there was anything I disliked . . .' And their prejudices settled comfortably into place, ready for home.

'By the way,' murmured the Chief, when they had both

closed their eyes for a doze, 'did anybody mention what happened to the gun?'

'No,' said Jeffreys, keeping his eyes shut, 'but it'll probably have turned up by now.'

ONLY AFTER provoking tears in her mother and some stern words from the Captain did Giovanna reluctantly lead Carabiniere Bacci, and no one else, to the hiding-place in the back of a little toy cupboard where she had placed her treasure, wrapped in a comic.

She watched him apprehensively as he unwrapped it and then opened it up and looked at her. Without a word, she tipped the bullets out of the front pocket of her track suit.

To the Captain's questions, whether she had known all along where the gun was, was that how she knew what the loud bang meant, had she, in fact, been woken by the door before hearing it a second time, she responded with bright-eyed silence.

Letting them out, Signora Cipriani asked the Captain, 'You couldn't . . . let me know? I mean about what happens to the cleaner . . . ? He seemed so . . . I don't know, but if there's anything I can do to help . . . poor man—and poor Martha . . . I should be at the hospital now but Vincenzo . . . he had a client to see, so . . .'

'That's very kind of you, Signora,' said the Captain, mentally consigning Vincenzo to the Inferno, 'I'll certainly . . .' He felt the solemn innocent eyes of Carabiniere Bacci upon him, 'I'll certainly try and keep you informed. If I'm too busy myself I can send a Brigadier . . .'

'Thank you . . . good night . . .'

'Good night, Signora.'

Outside, Carabiniere Bacci watched the Captain leave in his car, wishing that he too were being driven to the Officers'

Club for dinner and wondering why the Captain looked so bleak about it. Carabiniere Bacci was exhausted but he couldn't face going home yet.

He crossed the little Piazza and walked past Pitti toward the Ponte Vecchio, unconsciously following the route of the cleaner on that disastrous night. He walked slowly, absorbed in thought, taking no notice of the jewels glittering in the tiny shop windows along the bridge or the people who jostled him and barred his way. It was quite dark when he found himself in Piazza della Repubblica. He stood on a corner amid the moving crowd, vacantly watching the giant neon 'Cynar' sign rippling on and off across the skyline. The window of the department store beside him was stacked with red and blue skis. He let the pushing crowd take him across the Piazza toward the arcade of the post office. He couldn't shake off the fear that still sat inside him, as if he were the person in the cleaner's place. Because for half an hour he had really thought . . .

In the end, he had told the Marshal that he had believed himself to be suspected. The Marshal's great eyes had almost popped out, first with surprise and then with hilarity.

'You? Carabiniere Bacci, you're a tonic! I didn't think I could laugh at anything today.'

'But I was there, sir, both times, at least it looked as if I was and—'

'And the time of death? And your motive? And what weapon do you carry?'

'Beretta nine, sir, but—'

'Carabiniere Bacci, you're a young fool, I think I may have told you that.'

'Yes, sir. I know I should have thought of all those things but it isn't just that, or I wouldn't have told you . . . what I mean is, if I could have thought, even for a minute, that I might . . . of being

on the other side, instead of feeling like a policeman, well, maybe I'll never make a policeman. I've decided to give it up.'

'Oh yes?' Only then did the Marshal look up from his packing.

'Yes, sir.'

'In future, Carabiniere Bacci, you will give up chasing buses and generally looking for excitement and you will keep your eyes firmly fixed on the ordinary details of life—such as the fact that people don't go to work when their wives have just died, that you don't see a cleaner like Cipolla going about without his brush and bucket—that people wear overcoats in December! And you'll refer yourself to a senior officer unless you know you can cope yourself. Is that clear?'

'Yes, sir.'

'And you'll eventually make a very good policeman, provided you don't get over-excited and shoot yourself by accident first.'

'Yes, sir. But . . . the Captain didn't—'

'The Captain, Carabiniere Bacci, is a good man, a serious man . . . and he's been living in a barracks too long. It's time he got married. Now, get out. Your mother must be expecting you—and can't you see I've got a train to catch?'

'Well, Carabiniere, what can I do for you?'

Carabiniere Bacci realized what he was gazing at a lamplit bank of plants and flowers against the wall of the Palazzo Strozzi. The flower-seller was stamping his feet to keep warm, and looking expectant. There were Cellophane bags of mistletoe, tied with red ribbon, and poinsettia plants, red and white. He remembered that he had bought nothing for his mother.

He chose a red poinsettia and carried it away swathed in green and white paper. The lights and crowds on the Via Tornabuoni made almost an indoor atmosphere. The furs that continually brushed against him and the mingled heavy perfumes of the wealthiest Christmas shoppers gave him a feeling of suffocation and he made for the river and the Santa Trinita bridge.

Two black-cloaked Sardinians were playing the sad Christmas hymn on their sheepskin bagpipes. He stopped and gave them something. He wasn't feeling sentimental, just sensitive, tender, like someone recovering from an accident. The only thought that soothed his raw nerves was that there was one solid fact left in his universe, the Marshal.

'AND THIS is my second grandson, his First Communion picture—they say he looks like me and I think he does. Look at this, this is me thirty years ago on my driving licence, you can tell better from that—I already had a moustache in those days, of course, but even so . . .'

The Marshal's firm friend of ten minutes' standing had an enormous battered wallet of photographs and had been anxious to get started although the train was still standing on platform ten and showing no signs of leaving Florence. The carriage was already full despite the fact that the special trains carrying emigrant workers down from Germany and Switzerland had gone through during the preceding nights, unseen by the normal population. The Marshal was squashed in a window seat facing his voluble new friend with the photographs. He was content to bide his time. They had a night and a whole day before them and his own photographs were in his breast pocket.

An announcement echoed throughout the teeming station.

'That's us,' advised the Marshal's friend, who was a seasoned and ebullient traveller. He had seized everyone's water-bottles and forced a passing porter to fill them from the drinking fountain on the platform, saying, 'Do they think we're tourists who can pay a thousand lire a bottle for mineral water—do you know how much that would cost in two days?'

'*Express number 597, the 19.49, stopping at Roma, Napoli, Reggio Calabria, Siracusa and Palermo, is waiting at platform 10. Express number 597 . . .*'

'Waiting? Waiting for afternoon tea, no doubt . . .'

'*Passengers for Siracusa and Palermo . . .*'

People were still getting on the train, many of them standing, or sitting on their flimsy suitcases in the corridors. And all of them must have paid for seats.

'Poor Italy,' agreed the talkative traveler, catching the Marshal's glance rolling in the direction of these unfortunates, 'you need patience, that's what you need. Look at that couple in the corner.'

A diminutive pair, husband and wife, both gray-haired but it was difficult to tell their age.

'You wouldn't believe how long they've been traveling to look at them. I only got on at Valenciennes but they've come down from Germany—he works there, I managed to find that much out—but they missed a connection somewhere and they hadn't the faintest idea what to do. I think they've spent at least one night sitting bolt upright, just like they are now, on some waiting-room bench. It's a hard life . . . and I bet you that when we put the lights out tonight they don't budge. They'll sit like that till they get to Reggio Calabria, that's where they come from, I got that out of them . . . Me, I like to make myself comfortable . . .'

The Marshal didn't see how he was going to manage it. Their knees were jammed together and four large women separated them from the silent couple in the other corner.

'And I know for a fact,' continued his friend in a whisper, 'that they've run out of food. I suppose they only brought just so much—they won't take any off me, I've offered . . .'

The Marshal, too, had his loaf and a waxed paper full of black olives.

'*Express number 597 for Palermo is leaving platform 10. Eleven minutes late. Express number 597 . . .*'

'Could be worse . . . I suppose you're going to Palermo, same as me?'

'Siracusa.'

A man was pushing a rattling newspaper truck down the platform, calling out: 'Landslides in the South! Hundreds homeless for Christmas! Landslides . . .'

The Marshal's hand went immediately to his breast pocket where his photographs were, but the man rattled past under their window shouting, 'Landslides! Landslides in Puglia, hundreds . . .' The Marshal's hand fell again. Doors were slamming all along the train. A whistle blew.

'I want to show you something now.' His friend was opening up his wallet again as the train set off with a lurch, making the lights blink. But the Marshal's big eyes kept straying to the couple in the other corner. So many people lived on a knife edge, just managing to keep going, just managing to 'keep straight,' but if anything went wrong, a missed train, a week without wages, for them it was a tragedy because they had no resources except their families who were as poor as themselves.

The small, gray-haired man in the corner had that meek, patient expression . . . and his hair stood on end, too . . . his wife probably cut it for him. The sleeves of his suit were too short . . .

The expression on Cipolla's face when he had left him . . . '*Thank you, Marshal . . .*'

Why couldn't the two in the corner at least speak to each other? It was their dumb resignation that . . . and it was a threadbare suit too . . .

'Is something the matter? Marshal? I haven't said any-thing that . . . ?'

'No, no,' said the Marshal automatically, taking the prof-fered photograph in one hand and fishing out his dark glasses with the other. 'Nothing at all. It's just a complaint I have, an allergy. It's the sunshine starts it off . . .'

And he bent over the photograph without noticing the other's amazed expression as he gaped from the Marshal's face to the window where the floodlit domes and towers of Florence were receding into the night.

Continue reading for a sneak preview of the next
Marshal Guarnaccia investigation

DEATH OF A DUTCHMAN

CHAPTER 1

'SIGNORA GIUSTI!' PROTESTED LORENZINI, holding the receiver away from his ear and throwing open his free hand in despair. Across the room, the plump, pink-faced carabiniere who had been about to roll a fresh sheet of paper in to the typewriter stopped and grinned. He could hear everything that the chattering voice on the other end of the line was saying from where he sat, and when it stopped he was still grinning.

'That's twice today and three times yesterday,' he said.

'Oi-oi-oi!' grumbled Lorenzini, replacing the receiver with a grimace. But he added, 'Poor old biddy.'

Last time she'd got him round there she had kept him for most of the morning, telling him the story of her life, interrupting herself each time he got up to leave to invent some new complaint against one or other of her neighbors. The Florentines hated her, she claimed, because she was Milanese. As she recounted the persecution she had to suffer, huge tears rolled down her face and splashed on to her tiny hands which were as thin and pale as a sparrow's legs.

'And I'm ninety-one years old!' she would wail pitifully. 'Ninety-one years old . . . I'd be better off dead . . .'

'No, no, Signora, come on, now.' And each time the unfortunate young man sat down on the edge of a hard chair and tried to quiet her, off she would go again about the quarrel that had broken out over her engagement—seventy-three years ago but it seemed like yesterday!—and the tiny hands would gesticulate happily, the moist eyes glitter with malicious delight at having recaptured her victim.

'Do you want me to go?' the pink-faced carabiniere asked, starting to get up.

'I don't think you'd better, you'd never cope. I'll tell the Marshal—is he still downstairs?'

'Yes . . . at least, he was still struggling with that American couple when I came up.'

Lorenzini rolled down his sleeves and reached for his khaki hat.

'I'll have to go round there, I suppose . . .' He glanced at his watch. 'It's going on for twelve, anyway. I'll take the van and pick up the lunches. Ciao, Ciccio.'

Ciccio's real name was Claut, Gino Claut, but in Florence nobody ever called him by his real name, perhaps because it sounded German. He had dozens of nicknames: Gigi, Ciccio, for his plumpness, Polenta—either because he came from the north or because his cropped yellow hair was the color of polenta, the maize flour they eat up there—and Pinocchio, for no particular reason, although his shiny, smiling face and slow movements were a bit puppet-like. His uniform never seemed to encompass all of him no matter how he adjusted it, and a corner of his shirt collar was usually sticking up awkwardly against his pink chin. He had enlisted with his brother who was a year older and looked just like him except for being a bit taller and slimmer, and together they were known as "the boys from Pordenone," always with an accompanying smile. In fact, they didn't come from Pordenone itself but from a tiny village twenty kilometers to the north, right at the foot of the Dolomites. Gino liked all his nicknames. His smile got wider and his face pinker the more the other lads teased him. He smiled now as Lorenzini clattered down the stairs. Lorenzini always clattered everywhere, always in a rush. Then a look of wide-eyed concentration settled on his face as he stuck his tongue out at one corner of his mouth and began to type slowly with two stubby fingers.

Downstairs, in the small front office, Marshal Guarnaccia's broad expanse of back entirely blocked the grille through which the Americans were making their complaint. A patch of sweat had soaked through his khaki shirt between the shoulders, and every now and then he stopped to run a handkerchief round his neck. First he'd had to explain to them, in sign language and Italian words of one syllable to which they made no effort to listen, that they must go to a tobacconist and buy a sheet of *carta bollata*, the government stamped paper on which all official communications have to be written. When they finally got back with it, sweating and furious after having quarreled with three bar owners who didn't have a stamp and tobacco licence, he'd had to write it out for them, laboriously eliciting each morsel of information by more sign language. Now, an hour later, they had reached the description of the stolen Instamatic camera, only to announce that it had been stolen the day before in Pisa. The Marshal, red in the face, put his pen down and turned away, glad to be interrupted by Lorenzini.

'What is it?'

'Signora Giusti, Marshal.'

'Again?'

But it was always like that; sometimes they heard nothing from her for six or seven months, then the calls would start coming in every day. Once she had telephoned six times in one day, and always with a plausible story. Nevertheless, if once they failed to check and then something happened to her, the newspapers would have a field day: "Ninety-one-year-old woman dies alone after SOS call ignored."

'Shall I go round there?'

'You'd better, I suppose—no, wait. You can speak a bit of English, can't you?'

'A bit. Not properly, but enough to deal with them . . .'

'In that case, try and explain to them that they should have denounced the theft in Pisa. They've had me pinned here all morning and I still haven't checked the hotels. I'll call on Signora Giusti myself on the way back . . .'

He buttoned himself into his jacket hurriedly and took his hat from the hook as he went out the door. He was a little ashamed at leaving the lad to cope—they would be furious now at having been palmed off with a subordinate—still, if he knew a few words of English, that might help to quiet them. But when he paused under the big iron lamp of the stone archway to put on his sunglasses he could hear the American's voice clearly:

'Because we were just there for the day! Why should we use up the bit of time we had there! We're staying right here just across the way—listen, I can't see why you should waste our whole morning like this!' And all the time the woman's voice lamenting uncertainly in the background, 'Maybe I did leave it on the bus, after all. . .'

Even without understanding a word the Marshal shook his head at the hopelessness of it all.

It was July, and the sloping forecourt in front of the Pitti Palace was filled with brightly-colored coaches, the hot air shimmering above them. To make your way down among them would bring your blood to boiling point. The Marshal walked across in front of the palace where the postcard-sellers had their stalls and a man with a cart sold ice-cream that began to melt sloppily before the customer had even paid for it. He saw two Japanese girls walking away from the ice-cream man, licking their cones and talking rapidly, and paused to tap one of them on the shoulder. They both turned to stare up at the fat military man in black glasses who silently handed them the guide book they had left on the edge of the cart.

No doubt, he thought uncharitably as he went on his way, they'd have decided it was stolen and gone to Milan to denounce it.

He made his way down the slope at the far end of the forecourt where the high stone wall offered a little shade, and crossed the narrow road, threading his way through a stationary queue of cars. Some of the drivers were hooting and groaning in a desultory manner but it was too stickily hot for them to bother getting out to argue.

The Marshal walked slowly from hotel to hotel, his hands dangling at a distance from his body like the overweight hero of a Western, glancing unobtrusively into each parked car he passed, glancing for a split second longer into those that didn't have Florentine number plates. Every day except Thursday, which was his day off, he checked the blue police registers of every hotel and pensione in his district against a list of wanted terrorists supplied to all the police forces by *Digos*, the secret police. He wasn't obliged to do it, and he knew well enough that terrorist operations were conducted from private houses, but he did it just the same. Sometimes it got results because if it was just a case of a meeting or a long journey they did use hotels, and if they used the ones in his quarter the Marshal wanted to be the first to know about it. It wasn't a personal vendetta but he had his own private reasons. Terrorism was to him a middle-class phenomenon which he didn't consider himself competent to understand. He understood people who were just trying to keep their heads above water and who resorted to thieving and prostitution to do it, and those who gave up and went begging on

the Via Tornabuoni. Young ones, too, who gave up before
they started. Crossing Piazza Santo Spirito to his last call
before lunch, he saw two of them slumped on a bench under
the dappled shade of the trees. The boy seemed to be asleep,
the girl listlessly watching a trickle of dark blood roll down
her forearm. A dirty hypodermic, a teaspoon and half a
squeezed lemon lay on the ground beside the bench.

'Morning, Marshal.' The proprietor of the Pensione
Giulia was downstairs at the main entrance in his shirt-
sleeves, watching the Marshal pick his way through the
squashed fruit and pecking pigeons that surrounded the scattering of market stalls, along one side of the square.

'Nobody new since yesterday,' he added hopefully.

'I'll come up just the same,' said the Marshal blandly, quite
unperturbed by the unpopularity of his little calls. The pensione was on the third floor.

'This one here'—the Marshal's plump finger pointed to
the last name on the register—'wasn't here yesterday.'

'Yesterday, no . . . it's someone who was here . . . must have
been a month ago . . . went off on a tour and asked me to
save the same room—well, I wouldn't want to waste your
time on somebody you'd already checked a month ago . . .'

'A month ago?'

'I could be wrong . . . or, of course, it might have been a
Thursday when you don't—'

'A Thursday?'

'I'd have to check . . .'

'Check.'

The proprietor was fiddling nervously through the register
when a door behind him opened and a jaunty little man in a
crumpled blue linen suit came out. He stopped dead when he
saw the visitor but then sauntered forward with his hands in
his pockets.

'Looking for someone, Marshal?' he chirped brightly.

The Marshal considered him for a moment and then said, 'You.'

The little man turned furiously on the proprietor.

'You cretin! You said you wouldn't let him in!'

'And you promised to stay in your room! It's not me who's a cretin!' The little man turned to the Marshal who was watching them both with expressionless, bulging eyes while telephoning to Borgo Ognissanti headquarters for a car.

'I only had six months left to do, d'you know that? Six months! I might as well have stayed inside . . .'

The Marshal said nothing.

When the car arrived and three carabinieri thundered up the stairs, he said:

'No panic, lads. Just one harmless chap.'

They looked at the Marshal and then at the little man.

'Who is he?'

'I've no idea. Even so, he says he's still got six months of a sentence to serve, and he doesn't seem to have signed the register.'

'Come on, come on!'

The little man was struggling and swearing violently as they tried to remove him.

'What the devil's the matter with you? Let's go!'

'He's annoyed,' the Marshal said, 'about having told me. He seemed to think I knew who he was.'

'All egoists,' one of the lads remarked as they finally got their man out the door.

'Yes,' sighed the Marshal, considering his little trick rather ashamedly, 'I suppose we are.'

Then he turned, leaned heavily with his big fists on the reception desk and stared so long and so hard at the proprietor that his great eyes seemed about to bulge right out of his head.

'You were saying? This person booked in a month ago?'

'Last night,' the proprietor corrected himself, much subdued.

'Nothing to do with our escapee friend, I take it?'

'No, no. Just a tourist. I just didn't want you to come up . . .'

'Of course you didn't. But one of these days'—the Marshal looked up and wagged a finger—'you'll be shouting for help and then you'll expect me to come running.'

His finger went back to the new registration.

'British passport . . . why haven't you recorded the date of issue?'

'Haven't I? I must have forgotten . . .'

'Was it out of date?' The Marshal was leaning toward him so that they were almost nose to nose.

'No, of course not. I expect I've jotted it down somewhere . . .'

'In that case you'll find it for when I call tomorrow.'

The Marshal copied the name Simmons and the passport number into his notebook to remind himself.

'One of these days . . .' he warned the proprietor again.

'It was only for a night, Marshal. No harm done.'

Out in the piazza the market traders were packing up amid a strong scent of basil and big ripe tomatoes, the smell of summer. There were only a few stalls because it was Monday morning. The artisans' workshops were closed for the same reason and only the bar, with its white-painted iron tables outside, was open and busy with the tourists.

The rest of the piazza was rapidly emptying, and new smells were starting to filter out between the slats of the brown persian shutters, all closed now against the midday sun; smells of roasting meat, garlic, herbs and frying olive oil. The Marshal noticed he was hungry. The last stall in the line still had one tray on the end of it with a dozen or so huge, furry peaches packed in fresh grass.

'One thousand five a kilo,' said the stall-holder in the large green apron, catching his glance and reaching for a brown paper bag. 'Here you are, two thousand the lot, and let's get home to our dinners!'

The Marshal fished two thousand-lire notes out of his top pocket. The lads could share them with him after lunch.

He left the piazza at the end near the church, and crossed Via Maggio. The road was already empty and the shops closed; it must be after one. He glanced at his watch: ten past. Then he remembered Signora Giusti, and paused. He could smell the peaches, cool and heavy in their brown bag. He was thirsty, tired and hot, and his meal, collected from the mensa by Lorenzini, would be spoiling. The street was silent except for occasional muffled sounds of crockery and women's voices. A narrow strip of blue sky ran overhead between the dark eaves. He thought of the tiny old lady in her flat, sitting alone, waiting . . . and he turned back.

She lived on the top floor in the corner by the church. There was a goldsmith's workshop in the ground floor left, and on the right was a tiny place, hardly more than a hole in the wall, that sold flowers. Both had their metal shutters down. He rang the top bell and stepped back on to litter-strewn cobbles, expecting a face to appear at the window since there was no housephone. But the door opened imme-diately; she must have been waiting beside the switch. Inside, on the left, was a door with a frosted glass panel in it and a brass plate beside it saying GIUSEPPE PRATESI, GOLDSMITH AND JEWELER. The flower-seller's tiny den was entered directly from the piazza. Nevertheless, the scent of flowers mingled with the smell of metal filings and gas burn-ers as the Marshal began to climb slowly up the gloomy staircase, having looked in vain for a lift. A thin rope, worn smooth by many hands, served as a banister; it was looped through black iron protuberances set into the pitted walls at each turn in the staircase. Each floor had two brown-varnished doors with big brass doorknobs.

She was waiting for him inside her doorway, and she began to cry as soon as he came into view, hat in hand, on the last flight. He was too out of breath to speak and made no effort to interrupt her first tirade as he followed her inside.

'And it's hours since I telephoned, but nobody listens to an old woman—I could be robbed of what few scraps I have left in this world—but that witch won't get me out! They don't know what it's like to be old and defenceless . . .'

He almost had to run to keep up with her because the straight-backed chair on castors, which was supposed to help her to walk, careered madly along the tiled corridor with her tiny figure tottering after it, chattering and wailing as it went. The flat was long and narrow, all the main rooms opening off the left side of the passage. The bedroom door was always open to reveal the scanty furniture inside it, but all the other big rooms, the Marshal knew from Lorenzini, were bare. Over the years she'd had to sell her good old furniture bit by bit. They came to rest in the kitchen at the end of the passage.

'Sit down.' The old lady had already settled her frail bones into a battered leather armchair filled with an assortment of crocheted and flower-printed cushions by the window. Before her was a low table with the telephone on a crocheted mat, a list of numbers written in large red print and a magnifying glass. She indicated the hard chair opposite her as the place where he should sit.

'And what are the sunglasses in aid of?'

'Excuse me.' He took them off and slid them into his top pocket. 'It's an allergy I have . . . the sun upsets my eyes . . .'

'Not in here it won't!'

It was true that the room was gloomy; the window over-looked a narrow, sunless courtyard. She must spend the day keeping an eye on the doings of her neighbors, sometimes trundling herself and her wheeled chair through to the bedroom to watch the busy piazza. Those eight flights of stone stairs . . . it must have been years since she last left the building.

The old lady was quick to catch his sympathetic glance and play on it.

'You see what it comes to in the end? Stuck here alone day after day and not a soul ever to come near me. I haven't been out of this house for over sixteen years . . . just sitting here all alone . . . day after day . . .'

Big tears were beginning to spurt from her eyes and she took a handkerchief from her dress pocket.

'But the woman from the Council comes, surely, Signora? Doesn't she do your shopping, wash and dress you, prepare your meal?'

'That witch! I'm talking about friends, friends who should visit me, not servants! Do you think I'd have allowed a woman like that into my home when my husband was alive? But it doesn't do to have standards these days. Tinned food, she once tried to bring into this house, but I drew the line there all right. I told her straight . . .'

She had done better than that, as the Marshal recalled; she had thrown the little tin of jellied chicken at the unfortunate young woman's head, cutting it badly. Lorenzini had arrived in the middle of the row, having been called out to investigate Signora Giusti's complaint about the youngsters on the floor below having their stereo on at full volume, and he had found the social worker sobbing and holding a wet towel to her temple which was bleeding profusely. Lorenzini had brought the young students up with him to try and make peace, and a couple from the second floor had arrived on the scene to find out what the din was about; the husband was a street cleaner who worked nights and had been trying to get some sleep. There had hardly been room for all these people in the small kitchen, and Signora Giusti, Lorenzini reported, had been in her element, alternately weeping and chattering, content to be getting the amount of attention she considered her due.

Even so, the Marshal thought, as the tiny, bird-like creature twittered on about the evil doings of the Council social worker, there was no getting away from the fact that she *was* ninety-one, and that she could hardly hope to leave her flat again except when she left it in her coffin.

'. . . Telling me I should be grateful! Grateful! That the only person I see all day is a stranger who thinks she has the run of the house, who tells me what to do and what to eat . . . she even cut my hair off, do you know that? My beautiful hair . . .'

She was crying in earnest now, apparently, although you could never be sure. Certainly, her hair which was fine and white and fairly plentiful, considering her age, had been cut off just below her ears like a little girl's.

'Maybe she thought you'd find it easier,' murmured the Marshal unhappily. He remembered that they'd cut his mother's hair after the stroke three months ago . . . but she really was like a child now, and it hadn't been a stranger who'd done it, but his wife. Was it possible to be still vain at ninety-one?

On the shiny yellow kitchen wall, next to a gaudy colored print of Pope John XXIII surrounded by a border of old Christmas tinsel and topped by a red plastic rose, there was a group of framed family photographs; good frames, too, probably silver. One of them was of an exceptionally beautiful girl with abundant dark hair, a high lace collar and heavy strings of pearls. The Marshal had been admiring it absent-mindedly for some minutes before he realized with a start that it must be Signora Giusti herself. She must have been used to a lot of attention all right, and now . . . There were patches on the wall where two other photographs had been. Had she been obliged to sell the silver frames?

'She won't get me out! I won't be turned out of my own home as if I were a nobody, leaving the place to be ransacked. I've told her I could be robbed, but all she cares about is going off on holiday—that's the sort of person I have to let into my home! That's the sort of treatment I'm supposed to be grateful for—but I'll not go and she can't make me! You'll have to tell her. Coming from you . . .'

But the Marshal had completely lost track.

'I'm not sure I understand. Who wants you to go where?'

Her incessant chatter was exhausting him. He was hungry and tired, but she was as lively as ever, the frail little body rattling about in the big armchair, back erect, eyes and hands constantly in motion.

'I've already explained once, if you'd been listening, that she's trying to get rid of me for a month, put me in a hospital while she goes off on holiday—like putting a dog in kennels—'

'I see . . . you mean the social worker. But this hospital—'

'Well, it's not a hospital, not exactly, more of a convalescent home. Out in the hills. Supposed to be cooler than Florence.'

'I imagine it must be if it's out in the hills—and you know,

Signora, this young woman, the social worker . . . what is she called?'

'I wouldn't know,' snapped Signora Giusti untruthfully.

'Well, I expect she has a family, has to take her holiday when the children are off school.'

'Then they should send me someone else, not shunt me about like a useless bundle of rags!'

She was weeping again.

The Marshal sighed. He couldn't imagine why she wanted to drag him into all this, but he felt sorry for the social worker who must be suffering this sort of thing every morning. He tried a different approach.

'Listen, Signora'—he leaned forward heavily—'you must remember that in a sense you're a very exceptional person . . .'

She stopped crying and began to pay attention.

'There are other people of your age in Florence, but I doubt if any of them have kept themselves in trim the way you have, kept their interest in life, kept their wits about them—you know what I mean.'

'Hm,' said the Signora, sniffing. 'Florentines.'

'There's never enough staff during the summer . . .' He was treading carefully. 'And nor are there many places in the . . . convalescent homes out in the country. It's a question of choosing who to offer them to, choosing people who are capable of taking advantage of it . . .'

'Very good. Very nicely put. And who chooses where *you* go for your holidays?'

'I . . .'

'And I'll choose where to go for mine! And it won't be a place like that, I can promise you.'

'But how do you know, until you've been, what—'

'I have been.'

'You have? When?'

'I forget. But I won't set foot in a place run by a woman like that.'

'What woman?'

'The matron.' She leaned toward him and explained confidentially, 'A southerner. You understand me. They're not like us.'

'We're all Italians,' murmured the Marshal, staring. He came from Sicily.

'*We* are. But not southerners. Some of them are practically Negroes. Or else Arabs. They won't work and they live like animals. Where are you going?'

The Marshal had risen.

'If you're wondering where to put that—I hope it's fruit; it's the only thing I can enjoy with no teeth, that and cake— but you'd be surprised how many people come round here empty-handed. Or else they bring me hard stuff I can't possibly eat. That looks like fruit.'

'Peaches.' The Marshal resigned himself. It was true that he hadn't thought of bringing her anything, that he'd almost forgotten to come at all.

'Put them in the fridge. You've brought too many, they'll go off before I can eat them. Over there, behind that bit of curtain.'

She really was impossible!

He opened the rickety fridge which could have done with cleaning. There was a saucer on the middle shelf with a ball of cooked spinach on it. A small box of sterilized milk in the door. Nothing else. He put the peaches in the plastic bin at the bottom.

'Not there.' She was behind him, leaning on the wheeled chair. 'I can't bend down.'

He moved the peaches higher up. Next to the fridge was an old gas cooker with a battered saucepan on it containing the remains of the milky coffee which the social worker prepared in the mornings.

'*She* makes it,' commented Signora Giusti, 'and I heat it up after I've eaten my meal. But today I dropped the matches. I couldn't fancy drinking it cold. I suppose you wouldn't . . .'

The matches were down between the fridge and the cooker. The Marshal picked them up and lit the gas. She watched him quietly, worried, perhaps, that she had gone too far since he didn't speak.

'Not too hot . . .'

She sat in her chair and he gave her the plastic beaker of warm coffee. She was a pathetic figure once she stopped being bloody-minded.

'Now, Signora, I'll have to go.'

'Wait . . .' She pulled herself to her feet and reached for her walking chair. 'There's something I've got to show you.'

She tottered off, rattling down the passage to her bedroom, the Marshal following resignedly.

There was nothing in the huge shuttered room except one of what had obviously been a pair of high wooden beds, and a cheap plywood chest of drawers. The bed had a dusty wooden cherub sitting on top of the headboard, raising a plump finger to its lips for quiet. The other bed with its cherub, the wardrobe and the dressing-table had evidently been sold. So, very probably, had the carpets; there was a bit of cheap matting by the bed.

Signora Giusti was fishing, with some difficulty, under the mattress.

'Help me . . .'

He heaved the mattress up and her tiny hand grasped a leather pouch. She put it under his nose and said:

'There! A hundred thousand lire. Don't tell a soul.' She pushed it back out of sight.

'That's my burial money. I know I can trust you. You're a family man. It's the one thing, now, that matters to me . . . to be buried respectably. You know what I mean . . .'

He knew what she meant. To be 'buried respectably' meant to be buried in an airtight compartment, or *loculo*, set into specially constructed walls, with a memorial plaque and an icon light in front. These apartments for the dead, with their rows of red lights winking in the darkness, varied in price according to their position in the wall, but they were always expensive. For those who couldn't afford them, burial in the ground was free, but not permanent. After ten years the body had to be exhumed, identified, and the remains put into a small ossuary and sealed at last into a smaller, permanent *loculo*. If there was still no money to pay for it, or if nobody turned up to identify the body and foot the bill, the remains were disposed of at the discretion of the sanitary department.

'You understand—' Signora Giusti clutched urgently at his arm—' I have nobody . . . If they don't bury me respectably what will happen to my poor old bones?'

She was weeping again.

'Now that you know where the money is . . . you'll see to it . . . you'll tell them . . .'

'I'll tell them.'

'I'm not a pauper yet . . . Oh, if you'd seen how beautiful I was as a girl you'd understand! I don't want to end up on some rubbish heap . . . you must see that they take the photograph that's on the wall in the kitchen, don't forget that.'

It was customary to reproduce a photograph on a little ceramic plaque to be placed by the icon light.

'I won't forget.'

'You're a respectable person so I can trust you. I daren't tell anyone else, you see, because of the money. I don't want to be robbed.'

'I'll see to it. Don't worry.'

How could he tell her she was years behind the times, that to be 'buried respectably' these days would cost her between a million and two million lire? Her precious little bag of money would only pay for flowers and the photograph.

There was nothing he could say.

'I'll have to be going . . .'

'But you will speak to that woman from the Council? You'll explain why I have to stay here and defend my last few lire?'

'But I don't come into it. There's no reason why she should bother about what I say . . .'

'She'll have to listen to you, don't you understand? Because of the prowler in the flat next door.'

'*The prowler?*'

'Yes, the prowler! Well, that's what I called you for! I explained it all to that boy who answered the phone—surely he told you?'

'Of course he did, yes . . .' He'd never thought to ask what . . . 'The flat next door. It's been empty for years, hasn't it? And you think there's been somebody in there?'

'I know there has. There's nothing wrong with my hearing.'

'Don't you think it could have been the owner?'

'Can't have been. When he comes back the first thing he does is to come and see me. I practically brought him up. I looked after him when his mother died, poor woman—of course her husband was a foreigner, you know, so . . . Anyway, the child spent as much time in this house as he did in his own, and I was the one who nursed him when he had rheumatic fever—called me his *mammina*, he did—at least until his father married again—so don't try and tell me it was him, or her either, for that matter—the stepmother, I mean, because apart from her being a foreigner, not Dutch, he was Dutch but she was English, I won't hear a word said against her. It was a sad day for me when she packed up and left. I never needed any social worker when I had her for a neighbor. If she came back, and I wish to God that she would, she wouldn't be sneaking around in the middle of the night, she'd come straight here to see me!'

The Marshal wearily followed the tottering little figure back along the passage to the kitchen, and there he took out a handkerchief, mopped his brow and sat down again on the hard chair.

Glancing at the list of numbers written large by the telephone, he saw the general emergency number, 113, listed between himself and the grocer. He wondered if she ever called the Police instead of the Carabinieri. Perhaps she took them in turn . . .

He brought out his notebook and a ballpoint pen.

'You heard a prowler in the night. When?'

'Last night, of course! I would hardly wait a week to call you!'

'Last night. What time?'

'First at just after seven-thirty.'

'That's not the middle of the night.'

'Wait. Somebody went in there just after seven-thirty. I heard the door shut. I was in bed. I'm always in bed by seven-thirty because there's nothing much to do—I don't have a television because it would hurt my eyes, besides which I can't afford it. So, I go to bed, despite the dreadful noise in the piazza that shouldn't be allowed. Anyway, a bit later than that—I was still listening because, to tell you the truth, I was still hoping it might be him or his stepmother and that there might be a knock at my door, and then I heard someone else go in . . .'

'Are you sure it wasn't the same person going out?'

She gave him a withering look.

'The second person went in, and not long after that there was a row.'

'A noise, you mean?'

'No, a row. A quarrel. A quite violent quarrel, things knocked over, if not thrown. Then one of them left. The woman who went in last.'

'How do you know it was a woman?'

Another withering look.

'High heels. Stone stairs. My bedroom's right by the front door, as you've seen.'

'And the other one?'

'A man. I heard his voice raised during the quarrel. And he's still in there. I didn't sleep all night, I just listened. I heard him crashing about, quite late on, as if he were in a temper.'

'You didn't get up? Peep out?'

'I can't. I can get myself into bed with a little stool and my chair to help me, but I can't get out. It's too high, and I've fallen I don't know how many times. Can you imagine what it's like to lie on the floor all night? One of these days they'll find me dead . . . I have to wait for *her* to come. She has a key. All morning I've been behind the front door—I didn't tell *her* anything, just rang you as soon as she'd gone—and I had to ring twice before anybody took any notice, remember that! Now then. What if it's squatters . . . young people these days . . . that house is still furnished, do you know that? And if they can get in there they can get in here, and I won't have it! I'm not leaving here for a month and letting any Tom, Dick and Harry lay his hands on the few scraps and sticks I have left in this world . . . and my burial money . . .'

She fished out the little handkerchief.

'Calm down now, Signora, calm down. You don't seem to have thought of the one simple solution—that the house might have been let?'

'Without anyone knowing? And anyway, he uses it. Only a couple of times a year, as a rule, but he never fails to visit me. And if he'd decided to let it he'd have said, knowing how particular I am about the sort of neighbors . . .'

'All right, all right. In that case, since you say there's somebody still in there, I'll go across and see.'

She followed him to the front door, rattling along with her chair.

The door across the hall still had a printed nameplate saying T. GOOSSENS.

'You see,' said Signora Giusti behind him. 'Dutch. His first wife was Italian. He's dead now, of course. It's the son who still comes. Ton, they christened him, but I always called him Toni.'

The Marshal rang the bell.

They waited some time but no one answered.

'Would a squatter answer?' whispered Signora Giusti at his elbow.

'I'm not sure,' said the Marshal. 'Possibly not if he'd seen me arrive. But I don't think, myself, that there's a squatter here.'

He rang again and then looked through the keyhole, but it was impossible to see anything. Perhaps the hallway was as dark as Signora Giusti's.

'The other one,' she said impatiently. 'The old keyhole, lower down. You should be able to see the entire house through it.'

The old keyhole was a good three inches high. He crouched and peered through. He sat back on his heels, blinked, and peered again. The hall, like Signora Giusti's, was long, narrow and gloomy. The doors in this flat opened on the right.

'Can you see anything?'

'Nothing.' He straightened up. 'Can I use your telephone?'

'So, you believe me now?'

'I believe you.'

'Even though you can't see anything?'

'As a matter of fact, I heard something. Is it likely that the owner would go off leaving the tap running?'

'Good heavens no! He turned the water off at the mains. Everything else, too.'

'Hm. There's a tap running in there. I'll have to use your telephone. I can't go in there without a warrant.'

'No, but I can. I wasn't going in there on my own.'

She wheeled herself round and reached for a bunch of keys that was hanging on a hook behind her front door.

'He left me a set. You see how it is? He was like a son to me. Once or twice when he's been back—always on business; he's a jeweler—he's brought his wife with him. She likes to buy clothes here; they're well off, you see. In that case he used to telephone me and I'd go in and open the windows, air the place a bit. I can't do more these days. Usually, though, he turns up by himself and so doesn't bother. If he trusts me with the keys it's so I can keep an eye on things, and I'm not going in there without you.'

She handed him the keys, and after a moment's hesitation, the Marshal unlocked the door without touching it.

'Wait there. Better still, go back behind your own door.'

He was certain she would come creeping out again as soon as his back was turned.

He went toward the sound of running water, drawing out his Beretta as he went. But there was no feeling of life in the flat, only of something being wrong. In the bathroom, water was running into the sink which was filled to overflowing, evidently partially blocked by vomit, some of which was floating on the water's surface. The contents of the bathroom cabinet had been tumbled out on to the floor, and there were pieces of broken glass and streaks of blood in the bath and on the gray floor tiles. The Marshal looked about for a towel and, not finding one, took out his handkerchief and turned off the tap with one finger.

The door to the kitchen at the end of the corridor was open, and he could see, even at a distance, that there was a mess in there, too. Going along the marble-tiled passage, he could smell fresh coffee. Probably it had been spilled.

There was a tiny sound. The Marshal stopped and whipped round. It could just be Signora Giusti following him . . . but she made more noise than that, and she was nowhere in sight. He began to walk back along the corridor, quickly, almost running. He went to the bedroom by instinct. The room nearest the door, like Signora Giusti's. With the handkerchief still in his hand he tried to open the door, but it wouldn't move. How did he know, as sure as if he could see through the door, what sort of thing he would find? Nothing quite like it had ever happened to him before. He turned the handle and pushed steadily but gently until he heard the man's body fall over with a soft thud. As if drawn by the same knowledge, Signora Giusti came rattling along the passage.

'What is it? What have you found? Is someone dead?'

The Marshal turned from what he had been contemplating and withdrew from the room to turn her away.

'Do you have the number of the *Misericordia* on your telephone list?'

'Of course I have, but what's happened?'

'Go and call them, will you?'

Quieted by his manner, the old lady rattled away toward her own flat, then stopped and called out:

'But I ought to tell them—is he dead?'

The Marshal switched on the weak center light in the bedroom, then one of the bedside lamps.

'I think so . . .'

Why had he said that, when before he had been sure. . . ?

The man, though young, was very heavily built, and the Marshal doubted whether he could lift him on to the high wooden bed. He got a pillow which had no slip on it and some of its musty feathers poking through the grayish cloth, turned the body over, and propped up the head. A bunch of keys fell to the floor. There was no sign of life, and the face was ashen, the lips blue. And yet . . . The Marshal bent and put an ear to the chest. Nothing. Maybe the pulse . . .

The man's hands had been slashed and impaled by pieces of glass. They were big hands, but the fingertips were highly articulate, almost delicate. Wrapped around one hand was the towel that the Marshal had sought in the bathroom. So, he had tried to bind up his cuts, perhaps, or at least stop them bleeding. There seemed to be no pulse and yet, still the Marshal was not convinced. Something was bothering him—the little noise he had heard? Could have been a mouse, something falling over, the body settling. But his hands . . .

Suddenly he got to his feet and strode out into the passage. Signora Giusti was trundling back in at the front door.

'Go back!' he called, 'and let me use your phone.'

'They're already on their way . . .'

'It doesn't matter . . . I should have thought . . .'

He dialed the *Misericordia* number and spoke hurriedly with the Servant.

'I should have thought of it before, but there are so many

other things wrong with him . . . It was only when I realized that one of the cuts was still bleeding just a little . . .'

'The coronary unit will be with you in less than five minutes.'

The doorbell was ringing urgently. The first ambulance had already arrived.

'I gave them my name,' said Signora Giusti, tottering rapidly to the front door. 'No use their ringing there if. . .'

The Marshal was back beside the body when the four Brothers of the *Misericordia* came in. One of them was very young, not much more than sixteen, and wore his black gown and hood self-consciously. He didn't look at the body but at the senior Brother, waiting for instructions.

'Can we put him on the bed a moment?' asked the Marshal.

'We'll see to it.'

The four Brothers lifted the big man expertly and laid him on the bed. The senior Brother looked at the Marshal, who said:

'I just wasn't sure. There's something . . . I called back for the coronary unit.'

'I'd say you did right. That's them now.'

The siren was wailing outside, breaking into the peace of siesta-time.

'I'll go and meet them—frankly, I'd say it would be fatal to move him at all, but they might be able to do something on the spot . . .'

The other three were taking off the man's tie and unbuttoning his shirt. He was wearing one slipper. The young boy took it off carefully, then stood back. The Marshal kept an eye on him.

'Is it your first time out?'

'Yes.' He was very pale, but calm. Occasionally he fingered the huge black rosary which the Brothers wore as a belt.

'Toni! It's my Toni!'

'Signora!' The Marshal cursed himself for having forgotten her. 'Come away; they'll do all they can.'

'No! I'm staying. I'll keep out of the way but I'm staying. If they bring him to he'll recognize me; he'll tell me what's happened.'

She wheeled herself over to one of the windows and tried to open the shutters with one hand.

'Help me.'

The doctor and his assistant had come into the room without a word and were making a rapid examination of the man on the bed. The doctor prepared to do a massage while his assistant plugged in a portable monitor.

The Marshal wrenched open the inner shutters, the window, then the brown louvered shutters on the outside. The sunlight blinded him. He had almost forgotten it was still daytime. A small crowd had gathered on the pavement. He closed the window and switched off the electric lights which were practically invisible in the beam of sunlight coming in at the window. Only then did he notice that the bed hadn't been made up. There was just a cotton counterpane covering the bare mattress which was visible near the pillow.

The doctor had paused and now he lifted the patient's eyelids.

'I'm afraid it's far too late,' he said quietly. 'It was you who found him?'

'Yes . . .'

'There's some response but it won't last. Apart from the heart attack I'd say he'd probably taken a massive dose of sleeping pills, and to try and pump his stomach now would kill him. Is the old lady his mother?'

'A neighbor who's known him since he was a child.

Actually, she's old enough to be his grandmother. Is there any chance he'll come round before . . . ?'

'Not much. Why? Do you think there's foul play involved?'

'Don't you?'

'I wouldn't like to say without further information.'

'It's either that or letting him sink into a coma.'

Signora Giusti pushed herself toward the bed, and the Marshal brought a chair up for her, wheeling her own out of the way.

'Toni! What's happened to you? Tell me what's happened?'

She wanted to touch him but his hands were covered in dried blood, the hair wet and streaked with vomit. She took her tiny handkerchief and wiped his face with small dabbing movements as she must have done when he was a small boy with rheumatic fever.

'Toni . . .'

His color, especially about the lips, was slightly better.

The old lady's shaky, age-spotted hands went on dabbing and stroking as though she could soothe away whatever was happening to him.

'Toni, it's me.'

It was as if the man's eyes opened by her willpower rather than his own volition. He was evidently unable to focus on any of the faces surrounding him.

'It's me, Toni, your old *mammina*.'

The man's lips and fingers twitched slightly. He might have been trying to speak or it might have been the effect of the drug. His lips were parched and one of the Brothers came forward with a little water and wet them.

The doctor, who was preparing to leave, looked at the Marshal and shook his head.

The senior Brother had slipped away quietly, and he came

back now with the priest from Santo Spirito. The Marshal touched Signora Giusti gently.

'The priest is here. But if his father was Dutch, perhaps . . .'

'No, no, he was brought up a Catholic. His mother . . . I dressed him myself for his First Communion.'

The priest unrolled his stole and put it on carefully. He beckoned the youngest brother, saying in a stage whisper:

'You know how to help me?'

The boy nodded and took his place beside the priest who whispered again, this time to the senior Brother:

'If you would find me a bit of linen, anything at all, so long as it's clean . . . and a little water . . .'

He was an old man and not at all perturbed by unusual circumstances, or by occasionally having to welcome or dispatch his parishioners in a hurry with the aid of a hastily rinsed jam-jar and a tea-towel.

A small jug of water was produced, a scrap of bread from Signora Giusti's kitchen, and a white damask cloth from the marble-topped chest of drawers in the bedroom. The priest spread the cloth on a small bedside table, laid out his silver containers and lit a candle.

The dusty shaft of sunlight from the one unshuttered window lit the bed and its half-naked occupant, and the small bent figure of the old lady beside it. The priest in his white surplice and purple stole murmured a *confiteor* and then moved forward into the sunbeam and lifted his pale hand to grant the Dutchman a plenary indulgence and the remission of all his sins.

'In the name of the Father and of the Son and of the Holy Ghost.'

'Amen.'

The three Brothers knelt down in the gloom at the foot of the bed with a faint rustle of their black cotton gowns and a click as their dangling rosary belts touched the marble floor. The Marshal's pale bulk was just visible, very still, in the far corner of the room.

The priest turned and whispered to the boy who handed him the tiny silver container of oil. He dipped his thumb into it and made a cross on each of the Dutchman's eyelids.

'Through this holy oil and through His everlasting mercy, may Our Lord Jesus Christ forgive you all the sins you have committed with your sight.'

'Amen.'

The boy wiped away the oil with cotton-wool while the priest anointed the nostrils.

'Through this holy oil and through His everlasting mercy . . .'

A little whimper escaped the old lady's lips, but she was probably unconscious of it, her eyes fixed on the Dutchman's face, not following the movements of the pale, dry hand that gently touched the parched lips and the ears in turn and then reached over toward the wrist she was holding.

'. . . Forgive you all the sins you have committed by your touch . . .'

The cross of oil glistened in the palm of the bloodied hand. The boy dabbed it away and, at a glance from the priest, moved down the bed to uncover the feet, rolling back gray silk socks.

'Through this holy oil . . .'

The old lady's eyes never left the dying man's face. Perhaps she was seeing not the man but the little boy she had nursed through his fever long ago.

The half-lit room was musty and airless, and the Marshal, who had not eaten or drunk for many hours, felt his mouth uncomfortably dry. He ought to be formulating a report in his mind, but the stillness of the room and the priest's rhythmic movements and droning voice were hypnotic. The noise of children and dogs running round in the piazza below came from another world where people were waking from their siesta and going about their business.

'For the sins you have committed . . .'

'Amen.'

The priest wiped his thumb on the small piece of bread and held his hands over a silver bowl to let the boy pour a trickle of water over them.

'Our Father . . .' He continued the prayer silently, and the only movement was of dust revolving in the shaft of sunlight, until he raised his head and continued aloud: 'And lead us not into temptation.'

'But deliver us from evil.'

Another rustle and a faint chink as the Brothers got to their feet. It was over. The priest and the boy were quietly packing everything they had used, including the scrap of bread and the stained cotton-wool which had to be taken back to the church and burnt. There was no sound or sign from the Dutchman who must surely die any minute. The Marshal slipped out of the bedroom, hoping to find a telephone in one of the other rooms. It was obvious that this wasn't going to be a job an NCO could deal with and he would have to telephone Headquarters who would send an officer to take charge. He found a phone in the sitting room where the white shapes of dust-sheeted furniture were visible in the shuttered gloom. The line was dead and he had to creep back into the bedroom to get the keys to Signora Giusti's flat.

'Hello? Guarnaccia, stazione Pitti . . . yes, again . . .'

But that first call, from the Pensione Giulia, seemed to have happened in another age, so strongly did the dying man dominate everyone and everything in his immediate surroundings.

'And you'll inform the Public Prosecutor? Yes . . . no, there's no need; the *Misericordia* will take him straight to the Medico-Legal Institute. And there's no great hurry . . .' He didn't want the whole bustling crew turning up before the poor man was even dead. Although perhaps by now . . .

But the Dutchman was still alive. The priest had left and the senior Brother was sitting beside the bed holding one of the dying man's arms while Signora Giusti held the other. The Marshal came and stood beside her, wondering whether, at her age, she could take all this upset.

'Signora . . .'

'I'm all right. Leave me here with him.'

Perhaps this time he recognized her voice. He couldn't have seen her for his eyes remained closed, but he spoke suddenly in a firm, almost normal voice:

'*Mammina?*'

'I'm here. I'm right beside you. You're going to be all right.'

'It wasn't her.' There was silence for a while. Then he said wearily, 'Pain . . .' Shortly after that, one eye opened slightly and stayed open while his last faint breath rattled weakly in his throat and stopped.

PASSPORT TO CRIME
TRAVEL THE WORLD FOR $9.99

The first books in our most popular series are available in a new paperback edition for only $9.99!

ENGLAND

THE LAST DETECTIVE
Peter Lovesey
ISBN: 978-1-61695-081-1

PARIS

MURDER IN THE MARAIS
Cara Black
ISBN: 978-1-56947-999-5

WWII BERLIN

ZOO STATION
David Downing
ISBN: 978-1-61695-348-5

WWII EUROPE

BILLY BOYLE
James R. Benn
ISBN: 978-1-61695-355-3

SWEDEN

DETECTIVE INSPECTOR HUSS
Helene Tursten
ISBN: 978-1-61695-111-5

SOUTH KOREA

JADE LADY BURNING
Martin Limón
ISBN: 978-1-61695-090-3